Stolen Soul

In the Beginning…

S.R. McDaniel

PublishAmerica
Baltimore

First printing

Hardcover 978-1-4512-0015-7
Softcover 978-1-4489-5531-2
PAperback 978-1-4512-5321-4
PUBLISHED BY PUBLISHAMERICA, LLLP
www.publishamerica.com
Baltimore

Printed in the United States of America

for Jon

Contents

Acknowledgements

Thanks to Christa my kooky editor, who can brilliantly make sense of my madness; to Spencer, my literary consultant and contributor; to Kelly, my artistic consultant and contributor; to Stephanie, who really did sing Amazing Grace shortly after being baptized in Beijing. To Cai, Song, Alex, Kate, and all of our friends at the University of North Texas; To Vanessa for her outstanding Hong Kong ghost stories; To Juha Korhonen for the use of his font, his work is awesome www.juhakorhonen.com; To Seventh Sanctum, who possess some of the most helpful and creative generators around, www.seventhsanctum.com; to Jack and Judy, my inspiration for the Angels on the beach;

And to Jesus; for all of this is to His glory.

Romans 10:13 (NIV)

13 "Everyone who calls on the name of the Lord will be saved.

1. In the Beginning

"In the beginning was the Word,"...It all began with the best intentions. Anyone who has read scripture understands that in God's world there are many "beginnings". To a great extent it is as natural as the forbidden fruit itself, because there was evil and darkness as much in the beginning as there is today..

On the face of it, this is the story of a psychopathic serial killer who calls himself Preacher; who came into the world

with the sole objective to destroy. But it didn't begin there, nor does it end there. We are all sinners. And without salvation, the punishment for sin is death—regardless of the nature or gravity of the sin. So you see, we're really no different than Preacher...we all started with good intentions. The story is in what happens from there.

As is so often the case, God took something so dark and so evil and used it for his glory.

I began Book 1 of this trilogy in June 2009 in Hong Kong, secluded in a small hotel room, with nothing more than my laptop, my mind, and the knowledge that I am sinner who is forgiven daily. During this time, I spent hours thinking about my friend Jon. We'd had so many in-depth exchanges and conversations, so much laughter and good times, and eventually so many tears of pain and joy alike. But then, he died. Not in the physical sense, as he was probably in better shape than he had been in years, but rather in the spiritual sense. He longed for spiritual direction where none was to be found. After a long period of darkness, in a turn of events orchestrated only as God can, his reconciliation took place. After many days of solitude and prayer on bended knee, he experienced a life altering conversion. I witnessed his baptism not long ago. In a sense he rose again and left it all behind for a life with Jesus.

In Stolen Soul, Preacher experiences a similar level of oneness with God; it is a literal life changing dialog with Jesus. Although his sins are far more impactful and menacing to society, his witness to Gods' love and grace is ever powerful, ever present, and everlasting.

Come journey with me through a maze darkness and light, where the lessons of life are ethereal, supernatural, and driven by the Holy Spirit.

SR McDaniel—February 2010—Dallas, Texas

2. The Interview

St. Louis—The Belgium Cathedral

Sunday January 11, 2007 8:01 p.m.

The house lights splashed an amber glow across the stage, casting shadows that gave the beautiful, old cathedral an even greater sense of depth and richness. The large venue was stately, yet not enormous, just big enough to maintain intimacy with an audience.

Long abandoned as an active cathedral, it sat empty and idle for a number of years and had become the helpless target of vandalism and urban blight. Yet restoration always seemed imminent, and after years of planning and fundraising the Belgium Cathedral was restored to its original glory. Since then, it had been used for a variety of things such as entertainment, stage plays, lectures, etc.

Known from its' origins as *La Cathédrale de la Belgique,* or the Belgium Cathedral, the Gothic style facility was odd in shape and size. It was 144 feet square, 78 feet high, and 168 feet from the stage to the back of the balcony. There was also an orchestra pit which measured 48 feet deep and 84 feet wide, while the proscenium arch of the stage was approximately 60 feet wide. In all, it seated about 1200 people.

The intricate trim was hand carved oak and stained in a rich, dark walnut. The wall murals had been restored to their original period style and were designed to be shaded dark at the floor level and gradually grow lighter approached the ceiling.

Unfortunately, the cathedral had its share of darkness. Infamous, yet rarely told stories of death. The most notorious of these was the supposed internment of more than 10 generations of members of The Tinsley family. In 1918, the catacombs of The Belgium Cathedral that lay far beneath the streets of the city was used for the disposal of the countless people who had died of influenza; they were placed on top of each other and were buried in the so called 'ditch'. The catacombs had long since closed to the public but supposedly hidden tunnels connected them to other unknown crypts. It is often said that spirits roam the hallways of the empty cathedral; folklore provided a good back drop for this and most people took the stories in stride.

With the house lights on, there was a fury of last minute activity on the semi darkened stage. The marking for stage entry and exits had been well placed, the necessary candle power long since established to broadcast a televised event, and all was prepared for a remarkable evening.

Outside the cathedral there were various remote TV trucks, as well as a rush of last minute arrivals for the lecture. The excitement and anticipation, like a child waiting for Christmas morning, created an anxiety for all of those trying to get their tickets. No one wanted to miss any of it.

Rose was the event coordinator, the tour director of sorts and the calm behind-the-scenes voice that made everything seem okay. In her early forties and straight out of New York, her flamboyant personality and heavy Yonkers accent droned in such a way that it made you feel good about the fact that your life was in a state of turmoil. She was a dynamo that only knew the call of a forward charge, and never retreated as she made it her business to take care of everyone she touched. And touch she did. She was incapable of holding a conversation without the use of her hands; either in a touching or in a gesturing way. Her intention was good and never brought any harm, and in a small way Rose really did touch the lives of many people.

She was about 5'2", with a medium build, long straight dark hair, and artificial nails with a French manicure and a frosty top coat for special effect. She typically wore a black pant suit, 4" stilettos and a starched white blouse that she compulsively pulled on and played with the collars.

Adjacent to the cathedral stood a massive block of apartments called the St. Germaine House. These were constructed in a similar building style and period as the cathedral, complementing the ambience of the neighborhood. There was a line of mature trees in the front of the building, which hid a well used foot path from the street; uneven, rutted, and accidental in its design.

Because of the hustle and bustle of the media services, no one paid much attention to the footpath, what stood across the street, or what was happening in the sky.

The road in front of the apartment was said to be haunted by a headless black dog. In the 1970's the local newspaper interviewed the manager, who had lived there for some time. He claimed to have seen the dog multiple times—stating that it moved quickly and silently, came close enough to be felt, and then suddenly was gone.

There was an odd formation of clouds that seemed to gather in a storm like fashion. Given the time of day, it cast a rust color across the sky. Suddenly as if on cue, there was a single lightning strike which caused the street lamps to flicker, buzz and fade off for just an instant. An eerie silence ensued, broken only by the sound of an empty aluminum can rolling down the street, and a dog barking in the distance.

There was a single silhouette that emerged from the footpath. A dark figure: a man, not large, not slight, but there nonetheless. He wore a second-hand black, hooded sweatshirt with a faded back print that said: "I am the person your parents warned you about…" Even as he lit a cigarette there was little to reveal about his appearance except for the cross tattooed on his forearm. He wore his hood up while looking down, and when he did glance up his clear, bright blue eyes pierced the night. He was seeking something or someone very specific. He was not dispatched to see the event, to embrace its knowledge, or to achieve any sense of enlightenment, but rather his agenda was much darker than that.

Suddenly, a wind gust agitated the nearby trees and shrubs causing them to sway back and forth. As fast as it had begun, the wind stopped and the strange man suddenly vanished into the night leaving behind only the lingering smell of cigarette smoke.

Inside the cathedral, the familiar murmur of the audience, soft and unintelligible, subsided as the house lights faded to dark and the stage lights began to come up. The center of the stage was set with a black leather sofa and chair and a coffee table with water and glasses on it. The TV cameras rotated and focused panning for the right shot, the director began his countdown from five, and gradually the stage lights came to life.

Dr. David Teplitz walked slowly from the right side of the stage into view and the audience began to acknowledge him with warm applause. He was an older gentleman who walked with a beautifully designed cane. Simultaneously, a younger man, Dr. Matthew Reiber, approached the stage from the left. They met center stage, shook hands cordially, and the interview began…

DAVID TEPLITZ, Ph.D.: *Hello and welcome. Our topic today is "Psychotherapy and the Spiritual World." My guest is Dr. MATTHEW REIBER, who is a child psychologist and psychoanalyst. Dr. REIBER is a clinical professor at San Francisco University Medical School, and he is author of "Discovery Window—The Journey of ThroughSelf Children".*

MATTHEW welcome.

MATTHEW REIBER, Ph.D.: *Thank you.*

(The event was hosted by the American Advancement of Child Psychology, which hailed Dr. Matthew Reiber among its' top leaders. Over the last 15 years, he had developed a revolutionary process that would forever change the way that children with Autism Spectrum Disorders were diagnosed. The finding sent the medical community reeling. Literally, tens of thousands of children previously diagnosed, or misdiagnosed, now had another option. A different more meaningful method had emerged and was a considerable alternative. These patients, he diagnosed and termed as ThroughSelf Children.)

TEPLITZ: *Thank you for joining us this evening. Now you are one of the few child psychologists having embraced and fostered the theory of ThroughSelf Children, and as a result have made the transition from a traditional practice of psychotherapy to ThroughSelf psychotherapy. You distinguish in your writings that the only way to accomplish this is by accepting a spiritual foundation by which to base it. Was this a personal event that took place in your life or was it something witnessed as a second or third party..*

REIBER: *Frankly, it was both. Some seventeen years ago, I was invited to attend a seminar known as MindSync. The long and short of the seminar was that through simple meditational practices, a therapist could perform psychotherapy from afar, telepathically if you will, without ever seeing the patient—just knowing the patient's name, where they lived, and so on.*

TEPLITZ: *Sounds pretty fantastic. I am sure you were skeptical.*

REIBER: *Oh, I absolutely was. I thought the speaker was a lunatic, so to speak. And, of course, I believed solidly in a more clinical approach and that such business was nonsense. Needless to say, I was floored when I witnessed it for the first time...Keep in mind, that I was impressed, but not convinced that it was much more than a well performed lounge act. Maybe it was out of curiosity, I don't know, but I joined a small group and shortly thereafter began to learn some of the thought transference exercises. Of course, then it happened to me as well. During that time, within the small group, I was able to make contact about a half a dozen times with different people. They were in different cities and states; I knew nothing about the subjects and had never met them before. The messages and information I was receiving and sending came from a place that is not considered normal. It was such a mind blowing experience that it was the catalyst that started my journey into this field.*

TEPLITZ: *It goes without saying that professional friends and colleagues probably thought you had lost your way, as mysticism and spiritualism involved in your theory runs solidly against the standard set in traditional psychology.*

REIBER: *Unfortunately, very true. The official statement from the psychoanalytical world is that mysticism and spiritualism represent a return to a more primitive place, and is void of progression.*

TEPLITZ: *How did you refine this skill?*

REIBER: *It took time and practice. I tried many different rumination methods and through a process of elimination began to determine what worked and what did not, what the degree of effectiveness was, as well as a mapping process for a clinical environment. The results astounded me...*

TEPLITZ: *I believe that many in the field of psychology position themselves as rather agnostic in their approach to religion. I am curious where you were, at the time you began, and where you are now?*

REIBER: *In the beginning, there is no doubt that my approach was purely agnostic towards religion, specifically western religions. Once I began to uncover this wonderful tool, and realized its effectiveness, my belief in religion agnostically was replaced with a solid religious belief...*

TEPLITZ: *In a kind of spiritual/mystical sense?*

REIBER: *No, more in the Christianity sense.*
TEPLITZ: *Christianity at its' core was the belief that Jesus of Nazareth was the Son of Man, as well as the Messiah.*

REIBER: *If I may—is the Son of Man, not was. That Jesus is the living God. It is through that belief and the supernatural effects of his life on earth, his death, and subsequent resurrection that makes all things possible. That's the foundation...*

TEPLITZ: *Well, we are getting deep here, my apologies.*

REIBER: *No need. This is not an easy thing to comprehend, especially when you are immersed in a clinical environment.*

TEPLITZ: *You evaluate the patient carefully; telepathically or the old fashioned way?*

REIBER: *I actually prefer the term Thought Transference in favor of telepathy. There are 7 levels, if you will, that must be satisfied in order to insure that the client qualifies for this kind of treatment. This is usually performed in person or over the phone for the preliminary evaluation and that will lead to a series of sessions.*

TEPLITZ: *The 7 levels you mentioned, this is an adopted term for your work?*

REIBER: *Yes it is—but I wish I were the originator of it. I cannot take credit for that, though. The term was coined by a young patient; a girl who was 15 years old when I met her, during a ThroughSelf session.*

TEPLITZ: *Is this a memorable event for you in terms of your work?*

REIBER: *It is the most memorable, as well as the most exhaustive. It became the cornerstone for the treatment method.*

TEPLITZ: *As a matter of fact, the sessions were recorded and transcribed over a period of years. And they are part of your book, "Discovery Window—The Journey of ThroughSelf Children".*

REIBER: *Right. The weekly sessions lasted from 45 minutes to an hour. The client was extremely shy—and literally would not speak—she would only communicate via Thought Transference. It took some time, effort and coaxing but I eventually got her to speak in voice as opposed to Thought Transference. So, as a result I could record the sessions.*

TEPLITZ: *So how many of these recorded sessions are there, and will you ever make them public?*

REIBER: *There were over 250 sessions in all, comprised of hundreds of hours of supporting recordings. They covered a period of years, are highly volatile, and border on violent. These are prophecies or revelations that seem to represent a window into events that time should have long forgotten. They are compelling, almost hypnotic, in that they can provide a level of imagery and lucidity that seems like it is real; dark and filled with sadness, and one that has a painful history. Those feelings were revealed to the patient in graphic detail and the book illustrates them verbatim. You alluded earlier that our profession is one that was unwilling or incapable of embracing God in a way that compliments psychotherapy. I would add that when this notion is abandoned, the ability to implement this therapy will burst forth as a new treatment. As for the release of the recordings, apart from the detail in the book; you, nor the public at large, will likely ever hear them… and really never should. Simply put, it's best left on the shelf…*

Abruptly and without explanation, there was a loud, muffled blast; an explosion of sorts that rocked the cathedral, blowing out several windows. For that moment, time stopped. In total darkness, the audience gasped in alarm as they listened to the sound of falling glass …while the injured cried out for help…

3. The girl with no smile

San Francisco—1982

Dr. Reiber first met Sabra Torrington in 1982. At the time she was 15 years old, and from all outward appearances was a fairly normal, healthy teenager. But as was often the case, the outward picture was soon replaced by a deep despair.

His meeting with Sabra was prompted by a letter written by her mother, and judging from the description of her daughter he thought he could be of help:

Dear Dr. Reiber:

I am writing you hoping you will consider a preliminary examination for our daughter. We have read much about your work regarding ThroughSelf Children and believe Sabra could be a candidate. Although she is very bright (her IQ is 140), we've always known that there was something "special" about her.

We've spent the last 7 years consulting specialists.... . play therapists, psychologists, pediatricians, trying to find someone that can help explain her strange behaviors.

We adopted Sabra when she was 8 years old. Her birth parents died when she was two. She rarely cries, and almost never smiles; she just looks around with a blank stare. I was told by someone she was an "old soul", although I am not sure what that means. She never wants to talk about her birth parents or their unfortunate death. She often says the strangest things; like she "chose" her parents, or describes a past life when she used to speak to God regularly. She also insists on dragging us to church.

She told me things that she should never have known, and when I asked how she knew them, she replied "Grandpa told me" (he died months before she was born). She always has stories of 'old times' as she calls it, when she can recall places and people we've never heard of. Recently, while looking at photos of my grandmother, (who had passed away 6 years before Sabra was born) she told me 'this lady comes to see me often".

In one particular instance, I was awakened early in the morning by a strange sounds coming from the basement. At the time, we lived in an older house so odd noises were not uncommon. But this time it was different. As I approached the basement door, I noticed that it was slightly ajar. This was particularly disturbing because I was holding the only key to the door. I could clearly hear the sound Sabra's voice coming from the basement, but as I got closer I could also hear her laughing and giggling, as if she was playing with someone. Baffled, I went downstairs and approached Sabra. I asked her how she got in the basement and she told me "the lady" opened the door. I looked around the basement and saw nothing unusual. When I explained to Sabra that no one was there, she looked me directly in the eye, pointed to my right side and emphatically insisted that "the lady" was standing right next to me.

Today, Sabra is 15 years old.

From birth records we have obtained we know that Sabra was a healthy full term baby. She was also a twin. The birth mother had a very difficult pregnancy and lost one of her twins at birth. We have never told Sabra anything of her twin; in fact we were not even aware that it was a boy until we sought the medical records. Strangely enough though, she has mentioned 'that when I get to Heaven I can find the brother' (never "my brother", but always "the brother").

She has a very creative, vivid imagination and we often find her talking to herself. As an only child, I thought it was because she was lonely, but she doesn't seem to be outgrowing it. She now speaks about 'shadows' that she sees and tells me she has two 'guides' that are with her most of the time. She 'feels' people visit her but cannot see them so she imagines what they would look like after speaking to them. She is very fond of animals and tells me that they can communicate with each other silently. She claims she feels very 'different' at times. We know that she's had a lot to deal with in her life and want to help her heal.

We would value your opinion.

Sincerely,

Emma Torrington

Sabra, *the girl with no smile*, was a very quiet girl who did well in school, had few friends and almost no enemies. Her story was a sad one, and no doubt was the very reason why she was in such need. An only child, she had lost her parents when she was just 2 years old, and for the next six years was in and out of foster homes. She was eventually adopted by Tony and Emma Torrington, where she was welcomed as one of the family right from the start.

Sabra was tall, thin and awkward with beautiful large round dark eyes, and big lips. She had no idea how beautiful she was. Dressed in a wild array of colored clothing; she wore an orange flowered tank top, chartreuse leggings, and pink tennis shoes. As mismatched as it sounds she made it all work, and quite well at that. She had an artistic streak about her. Sabra, Dr. Reiber thought, was like many of the children he'd seen before.

Over time he would develop a list of common physiological traits that would characterize what would become known as ThroughSelf Children:

1. Large eyes with an intense stare
2. Exceptional fine motor skills
3. Introverted
4. Delayed language development—often learn to sing before they speak
5. Hypersensitivity to light, sound and touch

Of the many children he had diagnosed throughout the years, most shared one other very important thing: they loved the color purple. Everything they owned, from bicycles to their bedroom walls were colored in it. From Hair bands, nail polish, lunch boxes, backpacks; purple. In Sabra's case, she owned a horse, and although the horse was not violet, her name was. It has been said that violet is associated with mysticism, purpose & imagination. Dr. Reiber also knew it was an important color in its connection to the Crown Chakra; the head of the body as purported in New Age spiritualism. He theorized that their link to such spirituality seemed to reveal the following metaphysical traits:

1. Spiritual enlightenment
2. Sovereignty and mystery
3. Vivid Imagination
4. Visionary healers
5. Vegetarians
6. Feeling of anointment
7. Wise beyond their years 'old souls'
8. Intuitive
9. Strong connection to nature

Over a period of time, Dr. Reiber learned that many of these children bore telepathic capabilities that went beyond any reasonable explanation.

There was the story of the 10 year old Russian boy who had the ability to see inside people, as if he possessed x-ray vision. Once, he saw shrapnel in a man that was left over from a war wound many years previous, and described its location to perfection. He did this many times, under very strict controls monitored by the former Soviet Union, and 95% of the time he was right.

In China, there was a young girl who had the ability to speed up the metamorphosis of flowers and other such plants. She would simply wave her hand and the flowers would rapidly blossom. This would occur in front of many people, in broad daylight, and became quite commonplace. As with the Russia, the Chinese government was strictly involved in monitoring and recording the events as they happened.

Sometime in the early 1950's, the Chinese government recognized the military value of these supernatural powers and set about recruiting children specifically for this purpose. The idea was to develop a training protocol that would turn out an entire brigade of young mind readers.

Dr. Reiber was fully aware that the information he collected was anecdotal at best and that little or no research existed. It appeared that a common psychic link existed between the children in the different countries. Based on an overwhelming number of catalogued experiences, that connection seemed present early in the child's life. He also discovered the connection was particularly pronounced when it occurred in twins. It became obvious, even startling, that twins can have a shared experience while unknown to either of them.

A two month old infant became agitated beyond control, alerting the mother, when a life-threatening situation occurred to her sibling twin. As a result, tragedy was averted.

An eight year-old boy broke his arm and an unexplainable bruise appeared on his twin brother in the same location.

Seven year old twin girls were at different houses when one had an accident on her bicycle and badly scraped her leg. Across town her sister was driving home with her parents began screaming in pain and clutching her leg for no reason. After a short while she calmed down, and when the family got back together the parents realized that the twin was reacting to her sister's injury.

A man dropped to his knees holding his chest. At the same instant his twin brother, some 400 miles away, had a heart attack and died.

There have also been stories of twins who were adopted shortly after birth and were raised by families in different locations in the country and some in different parts of the world. In each case the separated twins were unaware of the others' existence, but they felt a longing for something that they couldn't identify. When they discovered each other and met, they found that their lives had an uncanny resemblance.

Their first meeting was in his office. As she sat down in the chair across from him, Dr. Reiber mentioned he liked Sabra's colors. She did not smile or laugh, she did not flinch, she just stared down at the carpet and said nothing.

He tried again and commented about her being a little shy—again nothing; just staring at the carpet saying nothing. Then she looked up at him, her large brown eyes staring intensely, and he began to hear her speak. Not speech in the usual sense, but rather through thought transference, or telepathy.

"I am telepathic," she started, her words ringing in his head. "And if I really concentrate, I can put thoughts into other people's minds, just like I am doing right now with you, Doctor. Sometimes, if Mom is going shopping, I try really hard to get her to buy me whatever I want, just by thinking about it. It works well when I want something like new clothes. But you probably don't understand any of this at all, do you?"

Telepathy is often defined as one's ability to transfer a set of thoughts from one person's conscious mind to another person's conscious mind. The theory had always been that telepathy was a spontaneous function that is subconscious in nature. So, it was rare that a telepathic episode was as controlled and purposeful as this. Furthermore, it was widely held that often such telepathic messages were dismissed as something of the imagination and ignored rather than embraced.

There was a momentary period of silence.

"Actually, I believe I understand perfectly well." he replied to Sabra telepathically.

'You heard me?" Sabra spoke in her natural voice. "But how…no one has ever heard me before…how did you learn…"

He asked her "if you learn something does that mean you have the ability, or the knowledge, or both? Like singing; learning how to sing will not prevent you from being tone deaf. Some things just come naturally, and all people possess this ability, but our logical mind interrupts the process, and impedes any possibility of actually utilizing the gift."

They shared this gift together.

"It is a gift from God" he stated in voice. "I suspect yours is too." She smiled.

She said she knew it was a gift from God. She also knew that he would bring a miracle and she would have her parents back someday soon. This, she was absolutely certain of. She would never let go of that hope. She refused to believe anything other than that, and she always knew that her parents were just temporarily away, not dead. Through faraway glances, with moments of silence that could almost shatter glass, she believed in her heart that Jesus would help her. She knew someday she would have her miracle.

Looking away momentarily she asked, "If it is a gift from God, then why are the voices so scary?"

He was puzzled by the question. The voices had never been mentioned in the letter from Emma Torrington, nor at any time prior to their meeting. It would not be until much later in his relationship that he would have any clue what she meant by *scary voices* and how they haunted her—but good bedside manner prevailed in the short term.

"Ah," he said. "It is difficult to say, but perhaps we should look for the answer together?"

And from that day, they began a relationship that would be the foundation for her treatment and eventual recovery. Over the next few years they would meet weekly and engage in an attempt to develop a program aimed at relieving Sabra of all the scary voices.

And then what *the girl with no smile* said next struck Dr. Reiber as so profound that it would remain with him for all of his life;

"No matter what, Dr. Reiber, it's all about Jesus anyway. His Love makes us who we are and reveals our heart. No matter how good or bad we think we are, we are always loved."

From that first meeting a bond was formed that would build faith in both of them and reveal events they would never have discovered on their own. Those revelations, her revelations, those that she held so deep, she would reveal to Dr. Matthew Reiber.

Those were events that had already happened, years prior, as well as those yet to come...

Luke 18:16 (New International Version)

16But Jesus called the children to him and said, "Let the little children come to me, and do not hinder them, for the kingdom of God belongs to such as these.

4. Born under a dark moon

Jeff City—1931

It was just after midnight, 12:03 a.m. to be exact. The weather was muggy hot, following a heavy rain where the breeze will not move, the air is thick, and no matter how many windows you open relief cannot be found. Such was the case on that night at St. Vincennes Hospital. In spite of the weather, it was the happiest moment ever for Cyril and Clarisse who would become proud parents to a healthy baby boy on May 29, 1931.

It was unusual that Cyril was nowhere to be found. He should have been at the hospital hours ago. A truck driver for a local warehouse, his shift would have ended no later than 6 pm that evening. Clarisse was thrilled with her newborn, but was privately worried about her husband.

The newborn was beautiful—he had bright blue eyes, clear and vibrant, that gazed about the room in an inquisitive fashion; the color of his skin was glowing and resilient, and a thick mop of black hair swirled about his tiny head. But he made no sound; no crying, no fussing, no fidgeting of any kind, and that would become one of Richard's trademarks. He would begin to speak late in childhood, but even then rarely, and only if pressed to do so.

Clarisse Crowe, earlier married as Clarisse Delong, was a half breed Osage Indian who lived with her family along the river bank. Other than that, little was known about her. At age 20 she was listed in the 1920 census as widowed, no children. Her husband was killed in a logging accident on the river, and was presumably drunk at the time. Also listed in the household was her brother (step brother) Hanley, 16 years. She lived at 201 West North Street, Jeff City—Her occupation was a saddle stitcher for a saddle company, and her brother was a heeler for a shoe company.

Across town there was a terrible accident. The locals, who tried to help, watched in horror as it all happened so quickly.

For reasons never known, Cyril decided against taking the same streets he had driven on so many occasions, and elected to venture down a new stretch of road. This road ran near the Alcan Lake region and was quite beautiful, but treacherous in some places.

His guard was down as he admired the scenery. Everything seemed brighter as he contemplated his impending role as a father. Shortly, he would be meeting his child for the first time. His eyes began to drift back toward the road when he spotted a young boy standing motionless just a few feet in front of his truck. Reacting quickly, in a panic stricken state, Cyril swerved to miss him while sending the truck headlong into the adjacent ditch.

Relieved, Cyril thought he had missed the boy. Trying to regain his thoughts, he could only recall the sound of screeching brakes. Suddenly a solemn, single scream fractured the evening. Dazed, Cyril quickly exited the truck and ran to where a man who was holding the back tire of a mangled bicycle. Both father and son had been riding their bikes home. The child was nowhere to be found. A few feet away an elderly woman was crying for help.

Only a decade earlier, most people knew him as Red. The six foot four inch giant of a man in those days had only one passion; playing baseball and Red lived it every day. But all of that changed after a nasty fall from Black Hole Mountain.

It seems that Red and his buddies had taken a little too much moon shine the night before, and as he stood on a ledge of the mountain, a chunk of it gave way, and he fell end over end some 200 hundred feet. Although he lost his left eye, he would go on to live a relatively normal life, but baseball would never again be part of it.

The child had been thrown on impact and he landed some twenty feet away. The father reached his motionless son and cradled him, wiping away tears from his face and whispering to his son that everything would be okay. But on that night God had other plans for the little boy; plans that would far exceed any expectation of a Fathers' love for his Son, and albeit painful and sad he died shortly thereafter.

Cyril put his hands to his head, leaned back against the truck, and began to sob uncontrollably.

"Do you have kids?" The father asked while picking up the lifeless body of his little boy.

"My wife is expecting any time now," Cyril mumbled.

"Cherish every moment as if it might be the last." he said with a quiver to his voice. "You never know when it will…now go be with your wife. There's nothing more for you here". He walked toward the arriving ambulance.

"Sir", Cyril asked reverently. "What was your boys' name, if I may ask?"

The grieving father turned to answer Cyril, pausing momentarily as tears streamed down his face, he replied, "We called him Don, short for Adonikam… it is a name from the bible. It means *my Lord arose.* Thank you for asking."

A calm came over Cyril, and a voice in his head kept saying;

[24]But God is kind and makes them right with himself. It is a gift. He does it because Christ Jesus paid the price to set them free. Romans 3:24. New International Version

Cyril climbed back into the truck, and as the ambulance pulled away, he headed toward the other side of town to be with his wife and newborn son. It was just after midnight, 12:03 a.m. …

In the town adjacent to Jeff City, another baby boy was born. However there was no joy or happiness, only sorrow and pain. This baby boy was born out of wedlock; an unwanted child.

Rose Alvah was 25 years old when she engaged in a romantic affair with a man. She thought she was different and meant more to him than the others. But he used her and when he grew tired of her, he moved on. He did not love her, and it made no difference that she became pregnant with his baby.

Born on that night in an old hotel room south of town, she wrapped the hours' old infant in blankets. Then she took the baby to the front entrance of the hospital hoping he would soon be found and taken care of. Only minutes later he was. Rose witnessed it from a distance and felt relieved. Then turning, she walked away never to see her son again.

The baby was rushed inside, where there were a flurry of nurses and doctors attending to the infant.

There was a single envelope with a hand written note inside that said:

"**My Name is Lucas Alvah**." The Biblical baby name Alvah means evil or immoral. It was just after midnight, 12:03 a.m. …

5. Stolen Soul

Jeff City—1938

Established in 1867, the large brownstone building was located near the center of the city and had first served as a mental institution. Although now known simply as a The State Prison, it was branded by inmates as Black Hell and housed many legendary residents from Xero Toleramo, the Spanish poet to James M. StRoseers, mass murderer.

The prison was appropriately named Black Hell, because of its deplorable conditions inside. Prisoners were only allowed to take two cold showers per week, lice infestations were rampant in all of the bedding, and skin diseases were common. Overcrowding, rats, rape, and the general degradation of prisoners were common. In 1930 alone, there were 125 suicides. Most viewed incarceration in this prison as a slow, lingering death sentence. Torture of all kinds was prolific and brutal. Food was rarely available and starving to death was not uncommon.

Perched at the highest point in the city, it stared down on the tiny hamlet, its sandstone construction blending into the landscape. A pretentious beacon of organized society, no one really knew its true character or the brutality that occurred behind its walls.

The massive structure faced west toward Jeff City, just south of the capital building. The front of the 3 story facility, a simple flat roofed box with windows was used for admitting and administration. At opposite sides were two buildings gable ends. Both were cell blocks: one for solitary confinement, the other death row. Both of these were in full public view from the brick road that fronted it. Outlining the perimeter of the 5 acre complex was a 25 foot sandstone wall, complimented by the strategic placement of 6 armed guard towers that monitored yard activity 24 hours a day, seven days a week.

On a hot August day in 1937, The Jeff Reporter issued the result of an astonishing trial:

Houseman Said He Saw Shooting Death in a Dream

Jeff City—AJ Houseman is charged with the November 1937 shooting death of Cyril Tinsley.

The vision of murder and mayhem came to Houseman in a dream.

That's what jurors deciding the fate of a 39 year-old murder suspect heard as the defendant tried to explain what really happened.

The 12 man jury had to decide the fate of Mr. Houseman based on the allegation that he had no lucid memory of the event, and only recalled it in a dream that he had.

In his statement to Dodson County Sheriff's Office spokesman, Houseman declared he had no memory of killing Cyril W. Tinsley.

He told police he had a dream while in jail days after the November 1937 shooting and the vision led him to witness the killing on his own accord.

"It was like a memory of a vision I had," the defendant said.

He said the gun fired twice—and he declared it went off by itself. "I didn't pull the trigger. I can't tell you who did, but it wasn't me," he told the jury.

In fact, he did not pull the trigger, but there was no explaining this to anyone, including a jury. In fact there was no explaining it all, because it simply made no sense. Sometime after he had buried his son Don, he began to get massive and debilitating headaches. They came upon him quickly, with little warning and were so severe they required bed rest. Typically, they would subside after a short while, and it could be weeks or months before there was another episode.

On one such occasion, his headache came on so quickly that he seemed blinded by an intense white light. He looked away only to lose his balance, fall to his knees, and in a tortured state his eyes rolled back into his head. He shook uncontrollably and tried unsuccessfully to speak. Unable to move, he lay prostrate on the kitchen floor and faded in and out of consciousness. Suddenly the back door blasted open, and like an invisible giant kicked it in, shards of glass and broken splinters of wood propelled in every direction. The lifeless body of A.J. Houseman began to twitch and seemed seem to float across the floor. First slowly, then picking up momentum, as if being dragged by someone or something into the darkness of night.

The next morning he awoke miles away from his house. The sunlight shown through the cracked windows of the damp abandoned building, where fractured rays of light were cast sporadically on the old concrete floor. The old warehouse district was known as San Pierre's landing. Long since forsaken, it had been a bustling center for commerce and trade in the 17th century; a multi vessel river port and home for many Creole and Caribbean immigrants. Although the fur and slave trade now long gone, many of the old buildings had been converted to upscale bars and restaurants, there still remained an under belly and those citizens carried on centuries old traditions in a quiet, unassuming way.

They were a people of Spanish and French descent, and their faith was known as Santoceria; a syncretic religion loosely defined by a Creole term meaning *one who works the Spirit.* It was a belief system that mixed and merged The Contracendas Religion (brought to the New World by slaves from the Caribbean) with Roman Catholic and American traditions. The slaves brought with them various religious customs, including animal sacrifice and the tradition of sacred singing. However, most notably was the ritual of telepathic trance used for communicating with their ancestors, deities, each other, etc. The high priests were known as Fathers of Divination and Knowledge, and He Who Knows the Secrets for those with a specialty in exorcisms.

At the end of the Civil War, one such exorcism gained wide acclaim. April 13, 1866, a young boy was murdered under strange circumstances. He was stabbed to death by his mother and father as they were attempting an exorcism to free him of demons. This all occurred at the home of Emile and Genevieve Montplaisir. The local constable found them chanting and praying over the dead boy. Both parents were practitioners of Santoceria. They plead not guilty to murder charges and separately gave similar testimony; each acknowledged they had murdered their son, but neither of them could recall actually doing it, as if it was carried out by someone else.

From that moment forward the Santoceria religion went underground, as it was outlawed throughout the region.

A.J. staggered home not knowing how he had gotten there or what events might have transpired while there. He was frightened and alone and somehow knew that only God could save him, but he questioned if He would; he doubted His love for him.

Perhaps it was the seeds of doubt; his deep depression, or the painful and internally destructive loss of his son, all of which resulted in a total abandonment of A.J.'s self worth. At any rate, he was losing his grip on his faith in God. The loss of his son would become so unbearable that his world, once full of faith, was replaced by his immense anger and hatred toward Him.

He began to seek comfort along the river, in San Pierre's landing, where the creoles lived; first with whiskey and prostitution, then with voodoo and witchcraft. He sought out the witches' advice for any comforting sign from his son, and would seek to make contact in séance hoping for a glimmer from the Other Side. None ever came.

It happened to many people; those who are lonely at heart, stranded in the darkest corner of their mind, looking for the company of a pretty lady. AJ Houseman had become one of those.

Mid-autumn in St. Pierre's landing was more like Carnivale than Halloween in the midwest. There were many people on the streets that night, most were either intoxicated or well on their way to it. The moon was full, pale yellow and close enough to earth that it acted like the revelers personal torch to light the way. The costumes were of all types and shapes. Some were ghostly and murderous, others were clownish and humorous, but all of them were completely off the wall.

The air was thick with a wet dense fog that hung over the pier like a worn out gray curtain. That Halloween night where everyone was in costume, ghoulish and ghostly in effect, he met just such a lady.

Like the legends and stories that preceded their meeting, she could sense his thoughts; knowing he was drunk and vulnerable, he was approachable and at an obvious disadvantage. It was in just such a tavern they found each other. She was sitting alone, sipping a drink…she was beautiful with bright green eyes and thick lips, and although she was in costume, her beauty was pronounced. He cordially introduced himself, asked if she was alone, an obvious yet leading question, and sat down next to her. At first there was mere small talk, the kind of thing that had little or nothing to do with substance and everything to do with strategy. Then the lady began to ask questions, a lot of questions. She was quite sophisticated, very sexy, and even the elaborate costume she wore could not hide that.

"How did you die?" She mused.

"Medicine" He said while pointing to his whiskey.

After a few hours the lady asked him whether he would like to visit her apartment and of course there was no hesitation. From the street level the apartment was quite normal and unremarkable. However, once inside everything changed. It was old, decayed and decrepit, and appeared uninhabitable. There was a sense of dread and he wanted to leave. He knew he was in trouble when he realized the door he had entered through had vanished without a trace, as if it was never there to begin with. Without warning her face glowed translucent purple and white like a ghost. Panic set in and he was engulfed with fear....a different door was opened...he found lots of people in the apartment, wearing what he believed to be old style costumes ... the most horrible thing was...he heard them discussing how they died...how they were killed and by whom... some of the girls said they were killed by their husbands, others by strangers, and he knew he was in a brothel of sorts.....He realized suddenly that he was unable to move; paralyzed in a sense...then he felt dizzy…eventually he fell unconscious.

In the morning when he awoke he was lying on the road just outside the apartment. He knew he was in trouble and needed help.

It was shortly after this that he met Miriam Broussard, a mystic, occultist, traveler, and occasional anarchist. She was born in Lyon, France on the 9th of March 1898, and grew up in Ile de St. Louis in a fairly austere environment. Her first taste of freedom came when she ran away from home at age 5, just prior to the family moving to America. After an exhaustive search, she was found and taken directly to the police station. It would be but the first of many attempts to escape.

Madam Broussard claimed that she was proficient at reading minds. So, it goes without saying that when she met A.J. she could easily read his very troubled mind. He asked for help and advice, and she graciously agreed to a reading for a nominal fee, which she eventually waived.

At first they made small talk in order to get to know each other. It became apparent that she was already reading him, and was terrified of what she had learned.

"There are many of you Monsieur AJ." she replied in thick French accent, while folding her arms. "Which one am I speaking to? Is it Runefire? Or are you Cursefilth? Perhaps you are the one they call Alvah, The Evil One?

"There's only one of me, ma'am." he replied. 'Perhaps you could tell me why I have the bad feelings all the time…"

"tis not easy, sir." she frowned. "You are a vastly troubled man, and many have come to call you home."

She went on to tell him that by her count there were 6 or seven demonic hosts living within him, and that he was in desperate need of an exorcism in order to rid himself of them. She further told him that he was very close to a line—a spiritual point of no return in which the control he had would one day disappear, and his satanic friends would dominate.

"Monsieur AJ," she asked with hope. "Do you believe in God? I think you once did before the loss of your son, is true? I urge you Sir; seek him with all your heart before it is too late. God is the only one who can help you."

He shrugged off what she was saying as complete nonsense. Although true he was devout in his faith prior to his boy's death, his relationship with God was just not as much a priority since then.

Then she asked him about the tattoo on his upper left arm. "tis the number seven I believe," she stated flatly. "Seven angels and seven plagues, no? But how it is used in the occult world, I do not know? Tell me Monsieur, where did you receive it? Have you no recollection of it, do you?"

"I ah, probably had too much to drink that night." he clamored for the right words. In fact she was right. After one of the nightmarish headaches, he simply awoke one morning and it was there. He had no idea how it got there.

"Monsieur AJ," she started. "In the book of Isaiah it said that God will create a new heaven and the new earth. So I ask you, since all believers will go to heaven and the non—believer will go to hell then who will stay in the new earth?"

Then, the demon who called himself the Alvah thrust the chair AJ was sitting in through the air and into the wall. It crashed into a million pieces, and a like a spry acrobat AJ leapt to his feet simultaneously. He took several aggressive steps towards Madam Broussard, clearly infuriated at her inference. She stood, with her palm outstretched and told him in French: "*Under no uncertain terms will you come further towards me lest you should expect a most painful death, and you are never welcomed again.*"

"I will go," He said in a gravelly voice that was clearly not his own. "But I will never seek your God."

Suddenly, his body language became relaxed, less aggressive, and began to violently twitch. His neck writhed like a snake slithering up a tree in a transforming dance, while the fingers on both his hands stuck out straight as nails. Doubled over in pain, he looked as though he was waging war within in his body. He was the timid one they called Cursefilth. As quickly as they began—the gyrations stopped. Suddenly he stood erect and it was over; Alvah was gone. He had changed, morphed into some other being beyond Madam Broussard's ability. She knew she was in over her head but she could not let *them* know that.

He became as normal a person as the demons would allow and said calmly while gesturing with his hands "Now, why so hostile? Maybe we should have a drink and relax a little? Get to know each other a little better."

He took only two steps towards her, but it was enough for her to react. She thrust her open hand even further forward, and like the force of being kicked by wild horses, it sent him flying through the air and crashing against the wall.

"Your offer is very gracious," she said with feigned disappointment. "However, it is one that I shall have to decline. Seek God, Monsieur AJ. It's the only hope you have!

And with that he left.

On that same night, he shot and killed Cyril Tinsley. Witnesses had reported seeing the two of them at a local tavern and everything seemed fine. No arguing, fighting or indication that there was any altercation, let alone a reason for murder. But the State claimed not only murder, but premeditated murder; a capital crime. He planned it with calculation and cunning. In cold blood he befriended Cyril Tinsley in the name of God, only to shoot him execution style.

Eventually Houseman, then 32, would later confess he caused Tinsley's death, but that it was an unintentional death, not capitol murder. Cyril Tinsley was survived by his wife, Clarisse, and son Richard.

The accused Mr. Houseman testified under oath that it was true that Mr. Tinsley had in fact accidentally hit the bicycle that Mr. Houseman's 5 year old son Don was riding. This resulted in the youngsters' unfortunate death. Witnesses at the time said Mr. Houseman was cordial even comforting to Tinsley who was visibly distraught over the accident.

Jurors heard testimony from many of the witnesses at the accident scene and all were able to corroborate Mr. Houseman's demeanor. All stated repeatedly that he was consoling to Mr. Tinsley who was quite upset of the accident, and appeared in no way to be angered or violent.

As the final summations were concluding, the State said it was unclear why Mr. Houseman's' rage was delayed, but that he sought out Mr. Tinsley, laid in wait, and shot him in the head. Ending his final statement with, "What other reason would he have to do so?"

In the end the jury of his peers agreed with the prosecution. A.J. Houseman was sentenced to death by hanging. The sentence was to be carried out early in 1938.

In February 1938 the last public hanging took place in Jeff City. About 200 people gathered around midday, on a day that was crisp and clear with cloudless, blue skies. One of those in attendance was a 7 year old boy named Lucas. Forbidden from going by the headmaster at the boys' orphanage, he slipped away nonetheless and became one of the generic faces of those assembled. Lucas had meandered his way to the front of the crowd, close enough so he could clearly see the men's faces with finite detail...

At seven years old, Lucas always looked like he was poor and abandoned. He lived in a group home called Pritchard Manor with about 75 other children. Although it was as modern and up to date as it could be, it was probably not a place most would voluntarily choose to live.

They weren't parents, not even parent-like people, only group home workers. They did the best they could but with such a high child to caregiver ratio, it was impossible to hope for a true relationship to develop.

With the exception of a rare donation, there were few toys for the children to play with. Most of what was available was not working or missing parts. Anything that was new was quickly broken because they were so many kids playing with it; junk really, all of it hand-me-downs. The bathrooms were unsanitary and foul smelling.

The home had 8 kids per room; the walls were lined with bunk beds and the whole house had a familiar institution smell; a bleach and pine combination. Anything that was of personal value became fair game, and was typically stolen if it was not well hidden.

Clothing was donated on a fairly regular basis. Everything Lucas wore was second hand and none of it fit very well.

In later years, he lived the life of a loafer and sought the Opium dens along the river. There, he lived on little or no food and only a diet that consisted of high sugar intake. His hygiene was terrible and his breath was foul because of his rotted teeth from all the sugar. His opium use would eventually progress to daily and it was hard for anyone to comprehend his existence.

But for now, every chance Lucas got to leave the home; he took it, even if he knew he would likely be punished for it.

The crowd silenced as the paddy wagon rounded the corner at Park Street. In the back were six men; all were handcuffed at the waist and shackled together; their somber expressions were devoid of any emotion; except one. He was the last inmate to step out of the wagon, while a group of local church goers began a soft chorus of Amazing Grace.

Houseman wore twice as many chains as any of the others. It indicated a more significant security threat based on his criminal offense or his mental stability. All shuffled slowly towards the gallows, staring straight ahead looking at no one. As he passed Lucas, the inmate twisted his massive neck towards him, peered down at the young boy with the blankest of expressions, his bright blue eyes piercing though the boys' innocence. Houseman's face was scarred and tortured; life had beaten him down and every ounce of anger, shame, and pain showed in that weathered face. For a flash of a second, their glances connected and the condemned man winked and gave Lucas a half crooked smile. Lucas smiled slightly in return, as if to acknowledge that everything was really going to be okay after all. The inmate looked up and continued to the gallows.

The death platform was a massive, custom built structure designed for a single use; to execute six men at the same time. By design, the stairs to the top of the gallows were staggered with short platforms through the upward climb. This would allow the executioner time to fit each inmate with noose and hood one at a time in an organized, systematic manner. During the building of the gallows, these platforms came to be known by locals as dead man's stairway; their symbolic ascension to a higher place; only to be plunged to a much lower one.

All of the ropes were successfully fitted and their heads fully covered with canvas hoods, amid a stunning and piercing silence. The wind shuffled through the trees, sending a final cool breeze toward the condemned. Suddenly, there was the groaning and twisting of wood, cracking in a tortuous manner as if it was breaking apart, and a loud thud that followed, bringing finality to it all. As all six trap doors opened simultaneously, the singing of Amazing Grace stopped and an eerie calm swept through the town. The wind blew gently, while the trap doors swung back and forth, squeaking in and out of unison.

The crowd dispersed somberly. Lucas however, stayed until quite late, watching from a distance as the guards cut down the man known as Houseman, his new friend. He somehow believed this man knew him and that they were connected. Soul mates, he thought? But how someone so evil could be connected to Lucas was a mystery to him. Houseman would be buried in a simple pine box in the prison cemetery. There would be no headstone, only a marker with the number 23451672; his prison id. Headstones were only allowed if someone outside the penitentiary donated it and years later Lucas would do just that.

He would never forget him.

Meanwhile on the other side of town, Lucas' paranormal twin was sitting at the edge of the pond on the family farm. Richard stared absent-mindedly at the calm water, which rippled when a catfish would quickly swim to the surface.

The 600 acre ranch was also home to several hundred head each of cattle and horses. As a widow and mother, Clarisse managed the ranch operation that she had inherited from her father, and made a very nice living for herself and her son.

Although she had a host of workers to help with the farm and ranch operations, Clarisse did not shy from hard work and had no trouble getting dirty in order to get the job done.

Richard had long possessed psychic abilities, but was quiet and reserved about them. He had been able to see auras since he was a toddler and quickly discovered how the terms green with envy, or red with rage got their roots. Seeing these auras with the fanciful colors everywhere, helped him perfect the gift he had been born with. This gift was something that he kept very private and rarely spoke about it.

He began to have dreams and feelings about things that were going to happen in the future; strange things that were not easily explained. Most of what he felt seemed to occur when he was a toddler, before the world began to teach about such things being unreal, unbelievable, and something to be forgotten.

At 4 years old, he was able to accurately guess what was wrapped inside his Christmas gifts and seemed to be able to finish others' sentences. It was as if he was aware of what others were going to say.

He was able to sense, feel and comprehend the feelings of others, including animals and spirits as well. Over time this was substantiated in his mind by the body language of others, and by the receiving of feelings from others. This became so much more for Richard, that he was able to project his emotions in such a way that he could feel someone else's pain or sorrow, fear or happiness. At first, it was a difficult thing for him to control and he became very frustrated by the whole exercise. As a result, most of the extended family believed he had "emotional issues." However, over time he did gain control and any question of his emotional well being became a distant memory.

His mother noticed things that seemed to be different about Richard, and although she loved him dearly, she had concerns:

—He cried constantly when others cried.

—He was always very empathetic towards others, animals, and even plants.

—He knew exactly how a person was feeling even if the person did not show it.

—He could identify precise elements of how and why a person was feeling the way they were.

Before long he realized that he had telepathic abilities as well. That is, the ability to send and receive thoughts freely from himself to others who possessed the same skills. At first, he was confused with random thoughts constantly popping into his head; thoughts of other people who were casually thinking about everyday things of life. However, over time he was able to focus his concentration and limit this kind of interruption.

The best part for Richard was that he got very good at knowing his mothers thoughts, but she always knew what was going on. Because of his gift, he did quite well in school, especially during tests when answers would simply pop into his head. His mother relied on him to discern for her who was and was not telling the truth, kind of a human lie detector.

But there were other things as well; things that he saw yet could not understand. He could sense things no one else could. There were times when he could see black shadows from the corner of his eyes, hear heavy breathing, or sense a familiar presence in the room. Sometimes he would feel intense cold spots on certain parts of his body, or be held down in his bed by someone as they whispered his name. But by far, the most extreme vision he had ever seen, was the one witnessed on that day; the day Jeff City executed AJ Houseman. He had no desire or intention of viewing the execution. He knew how angry his mother would be if she found out otherwise. Regardless of his intent, he did view it, He saw it all in graphic detail—from start to finish in his mind. With the execution, Richard believed the memory that tied his fathers' death to Houseman was finally over. He was certain there was a young boy; a nameless young boy his same age and identical in many ways. He also sensed that the other young boy was the son of AJ Houseman. He would be a constant reminder to Richard of his father's murder. Richard Tinsley would never forget him.

Revelation 12:3 (New International Version)

[3]Then another sign appeared in heaven: an enormous red dragon with seven heads and ten horns and seven crowns on his heads.

6. Lost in Jesusland

Caperville—1967

The county road was well traveled and in most places it was actually more dirt than gravel. On either side of it was acre upon acre of green grass fields for the livestock to graze in the hot summer sun.

The city bus from Caperville (a small town in central California) stopped on the county road only once a day, usually around evening. That day the door swung open and two hippies emerged. Richard and Mary Tinsley stepped off the bus, back packs and duffle bags in tow, and began the half mile hike to their destination. The bus pulled away, leaving behind a cloud of dust that seemed to linger in the hot thick air.

The San Sabena Valley was a vast rural region of northern California, just outside of San Francisco. It extended from Silegsberg south to the Cheppawann Mountains. Unlike the neighboring Silegsberg Valley, the river system for which San Sabena was named did not extend very far. Most of the valley south of Silegsberg drained into Alpine Lake. Major waterways including the San Sabena, Queens and Butane rivers had been largely diverted for agricultural uses and were typically dry in their lower reaches.

San Sabena County had a colorful past; legendary bank robber Marcus Phoenix was killed in 1873 after a string of over 20 bank robberies. A sole plaque marks the place where he was slain and oddly enough, it is located only steps from the present day local bank. The first post office was established in 1899, but was closed 12 months later because of insufficient use. It reopened when the City of Caperville was incorporated in 1903.

Happy in love, newlyweds Richard and Mary Tinsley walked hand in hand toward what would be their new home. A kind and respectful man, Richard wore an olive green t-shirt that had a faded Peace symbol on the back and a small oil stain on the front near the hem. He had narrow bright blue eyes; wispy long brown hair; and a snub nose. Mary, a lanky woman, was also wearing a T-shirt. She had wide brown eyes, long stringy golden hair that was unkempt, and a slightly crooked nose. At times she acted irritable yet eccentric and often displayed a brittle smile.

After a simple wedding attended by a few friends and family, Richard and Mary set off on their honeymoon adventure. It would begin in Mexico and then on to California which if all went well, they would plan to call home.

They were on their way to a place called Senzagas, not far from the port of San Valesco, Mexico. After an exhaustive 36 hour journey via plane, train and bus they finally arrived at their hotel, The Hotel Espas. With barely enough energy to shower, they collapsed into bed and slept away the next 12 hours.

The Hotel Espas, every bit as beautiful as the brochures had pictured, sported an assortment of accommodations to cater to each individual's needs. The brochure read as follows:

In the heart of downtown Senzagas, the Hotel Espas is the architectural centerpiece of the area. You will realize you are in for something special from the moment you enter the modern, spacious and colorful lobby. Perfect for meeting friends, relaxing on the terrace overlooking beautiful Cano Lake or enjoying the unique secluded second floor outdoor swimming pool with a view that transports you to another world.

Comfort is number one at The Hotel Espas; everything is designed to make your stay a most pleasurable experience.

The following day they awoke to blue skies, soft gentle ocean breezes and breakfast in bed. They had a whole lifetime ahead of them. The day would be full of sightseeing—taking in as much as they could. First on the list was the Cathedral of the Del Orphans, followed by the Cave of Dame Lal, and the Lost Tomb of the Ancients. Late that evening, after hundreds of pictures and a full day of walking, they found themselves on the beach. Holding each other in a tight embrace, covered in a blanket, they fell asleep to the romantic sound of the waves crashing softly.

The morning sun was bright, the ocean breeze cool, but the day would began in a way that no one ever wants. When Richard and Mary awoke, they realized that they had been robbed sometime during the night. Everything was gone, except the blanket they slept in and Richards' cowboy hat. Their pants, wallet, money, car keys: Everything. Strangely enough, the car was still parked where they left it. It was locked and with no keys getting in would be tough.

There was a sense of panic on their faces, the kind that creeps up on you when you suddenly start to believe that there is no way out. They were scared and had no idea what to do or where to go. The only thing they did know was that they were nowhere near their hotel. Not only had they been robbed, they were lost.

Out of nowhere came an older couple going for their morning walk on the beach. Jack and Judy were a retired couple from

Indiana. They drove their RV all over Mexico and said that home was now wherever they stopped for the night. As they approached Richard and Mary, they realized they needed help and that's just what they did. Judy went back to the RV to get some clothes and Jack got a slim jim from his tool box, opened their rental car and hot wired it. They gave Richard and Mary food and cash and wished them the very best of luck. When they tried to have a conversation about repaying the money, Jack and Judy would have nothing to do with it. They said it was all a gift from God and did not belong to them anyway. The only thing they asked was that they all join hands and pray together. Richard and Mary were happy to oblige. They started to leave but after a few short steps, Richard turned to press them for an address to return the clothes and repay the money. To their astonishment, their "angels" were gone. There was no trace of them at all; no RV, no kind couple. Nothing, not even RV tires tracks. Vanished; it was as if they had never even been there at all.

Richard and Mary made it back to the hotel fully believing that they had just encountered real angels and that everything that they had witnessed was by design.

Now that the worst was over, they laughed hysterically about their great "honeymoon adventure". Needless to say, they were happy to be on their way as they crossed the border from Tijuana into San Diego.

As they began the drive north, they decided to investigate a little along the way. Quite by accident, they stumbled across the Mission District, a 16 block neighborhood in downtown San Jaunito, California. It turned out to be a nice retreat from their previously stressful adventure, and they welcomed it.

The small Missionary outpost opened in 1867 when the land was purchased by private citizens hoping to create a new church center. Over the years the area experienced blight and urban decay, but recently it had been revived. The Mission district had become home to many festivals and gathering spots, and gradually became a magnet for a younger generation.

Richard and Mary were immediately attracted to the area because it reminded them of the Soulard district south of St. Louis; a neighborhood that got its name from Antoine Soulard, a Frenchman who first surveyed the area for the King of Spain. It was one of the oldest parts of the city and had buildings dating from the mid to late 1800s.

After a short drive down the old bricked streets, they found a quaint restaurant called the Capistrano City Grille and decided that would be a good place to stop.

During the leisurely lunch they talked about where in California they would call home, something they had yet to decide on. Richard and Mary had a lot of ideas and thoughts and bounced things back and forth, but nothing ever really stuck. After lunch, they went to the counter to pay the bill and noticed a flyer advertising Jesusland. When they asked the hostess what she knew about the flyer on the bulletin board they were pleasantly surprised with her response. She knew all about Jesusland, as her parents had lived there some time ago. Just south of San Francisco, it offered a comfortable lifestyle; quiet and somewhat reclusive, but safe.

Within a few moments, Richard was on the phone with the one of the Deacons of Jesusland, a man named Matthew. After only a brief conversation, Richard was convinced that this was where they were supposed to be, and Mary agreed. He asked for directions and began making plans to arrive at their new home later that day. They didn't know why but Richard and Mary felt like this was somehow connected to their encounter with the "angels" in Mexico. This would begin their journey to Jesusland.

After several hours of driving, they dropped off their rental car at a location in Caperville and with great anticipation they boarded the bus headed for State Highway 14. After a short hike from the bus drop off they came to another dirt road with a directional sign that said, *Welcome to Jesusland.* Directly below the sign was inscribed:

Acts 2:44-47 **44All the believers were together and had everything in common. 45Selling their possessions and goods, they gave to anyone as he had need. 46Every day they continued to meet together in the temple courts. They broke bread in their homes and ate together with glad and sincere hearts, 47praising God and enjoying the favor of all the people. And the Lord added to their number daily those who were being saved. (New International Version)**

As they made the hike up Searchers Mountain, they marveled at the breathtaking view of the lake. At 3100 feet, you could see the setting sun smother a broad area of the San Sabena horizon and a variety of birds flock to the lake en mass. The air seemed more crisp and renewed with freshness with each additional foot traveled.

Richard and Mary knew they had come home at last…

Jesusland was a Christian hippie commune that consisted of about 50 men, women and children. It was one of several thousand communes that existed in 1967. What began in the late 1950's as a cattle ranch, was known simply as "The Ranch" after the Hippies took it over and had been absent of cattle for a number of years.

The Hippy Movement was born in opposition to the Vietnam War. It was the result of a fracture in the system of values of a consumptive society and in contrast to the traditional family. It embraced Eastern philosophies and religions, and global pacifism. The hippies and later movements prepared the ground for the rebirth of naturism and nudism. They rejected violence and preached harmony, mainly for human beings and the planet Earth. Harmony became the mantelpiece of their existence: they began to form communes where the material goods and work were shared among its' members. One of the communal elements was the birth of so called *Free Love*. It was in effect, love (or sex) without restriction or commitment and provided relational living without the need for marriage.

But it was short lived, and many of the Hippies soon moved away from "The Ranch". Disillusioned with the failure of the communal system, they sought other life alternatives. Not all left "The Ranch". Those who stayed began to evangelize and preach a "One Way" belief system as New Christians who faithfully followed Jesus.

Armed with this love for God through the teachings of Christ, Jesusland (as it would later be known) would become a thriving, intentional, Christian community. Although it retained many of the communal values of its predecessor, they no longer practiced free love, drugs, or nudity and it attracted many as the ideal place to start and raise a family. That was the primary reason Richard and Mary had come to Jesusland.

The road ended and before them stood a monumental building that would soon become home. As they took it all in, they realized that what had originally looked like one building was actually a series of smaller structures with red tile roofs that were connected by stately stone walls. Built into one of the tallest cliffs on Searchers Mountain, it offered a breathtaking view of the ravine below.

Everyone simply called him Preacher. He was the spiritual leader and teacher at Jesusland and greeted Richard and Mary with a firm handshake and hug as they entered the compound. They noticed he had a tattoo of a “7" and inquired about it in a shy unsure way. He told them that it represented a commitment to one’s Faith through the sevenfold spirit and that anyone who had made that commitment was welcome get one. It all seemed a little foreign to them. Preacher took them on a brief tour of the grounds and showed them to their sleeping quarters. There they could change clothes, clean up a bit, and get ready for the evening meal and prayer meeting.

Everything seemed just as they had expected it, but it was not. Darkness hovered over Jesusland and evil came to call it home.

He was a mysterious man that most people knew little about, other than he came from a very small town in the Midwest, was orphaned as a child, and had only recently been released from prison; incarcerated for 10 years for a crime he did not commit.

On Christmas Eve, 1957, he and a friend robbed a neighborhood store of money, clothing, and other articles. The owner was not there during the robbery, but was informed of what had taken place. Based on the description of one of the suspects, the store owner was sure he knew the robbers.

Vengeful and angry, he hunted them. He told anyone who would listen that he would kill both men when he found them. Eight days later on New Year’s Day, Preacher boarded a bus at Maple and Raito St. en route to a friend’s house. The store owner, a Chinese immigrant named James, was in a car with another man when he saw Preacher board the bus. They followed the bus for 18 blocks and when Preacher got off at his stop, James confronted him with a .38 and jammed it into his stomach. He squeezed the trigger at the same time Preacher grabbed the barrel and jerked it away. The two wrestled as Preacher tried to get control of the gun. During the ensuing struggle there was a spontaneous flash of gunfire; the bullet hit the store owner in the heart, killing him instantly.

First the arrest and then a trial. Preacher testified to the story as it happened; that he feared for his life; that although true he had participated in the robbery there was no intent to murder. Preacher proclaimed his innocence from day one and argued vehemently that it was not a premeditated killing. His defense provided one witness to this who testified that it was self defense. The jury disagreed. They convicted him of reckless manslaughter and sentenced him to 15 years at Rock Mount Penitentiary, a maximum security prison.

As a model inmate, he was released early for good behavior and was determined to start his life again.

He wandered onto "The Ranch" a few years later, gave the commune the new life and spirit it needed, and changed Jesusland forever. From that point forward, it became a prosperous, lively, productive community, and maintained a spiritually centered environment.

Bible study and prayer meetings became an important after meal event and all we're encouraged to attend. However, what began as a simple offer to worship was no longer optional. Those who chose not to attend were reprimanded. At first the punishment was mild, consisting of menial labor for the good of the community. They were meant simply as expressions of disappointment rather than control. For those who continued to ignore the mandate, bizarre things began to occur. At first, those who were not Christian or had no desire to become Christian simply disappeared. The night previous they said good evening and the next morning their cabins and all of their belongings were gone. It was a strong, obvious signal for non-believers; any attempt at uprising would surely be met with an unfortunate outcome.

Then there were the "unfortunate" accidents. In all, 7 members of the community died over a 2 year period. There were always strange and suspicious circumstances surrounding the events. All of the victims had defied Preacher with their spiritual indifference, so everyone believed that he was the one who facilitated such things. No one dared to alert the authorities for fear they too would fall victim to an "accident". One drowning, two rattlesnake bites, two falls from nearby Searchers Mountain; one heart attack and one simply went mad. The message was clear: go to church daily and everyone did.

One by one, those people were replaced by others, and these became the inner circle to Preacher. Nothing was discussed in open as it once had been, but rather was first reviewed by the Circle, and then one of Preacher's so-called body guards would announce to the rest of the commune the latest decree.

The Circle, a group of 7 men responsible for insuring the by-laws were closely followed, were a dark secretive group comprised of some of the worst that life had to dole out. How uncanny that a new member of the Circle arrived at Jesusland each time someone one else went missing, accidentally or otherwise.

What no one knew at the time, or suspected and never spoke of, was that all of the men that made up the Circle were former prison inmates. Their past was sordid; a precarious lot with all sorts of background details that would frighten even the most courageous. Like a who's who of the underworld. Though never truly revealed, these men were now and forever a part of Jesusland:

Andrew Vawdrey: A cynical, inconsiderate man with very dark skin, green eyes, and black hair. Rotund, with a sharp-featured face. He was interested in children and he was a convicted drug dealer and prone to violence. The called him **Soriptor.**

Barnard Hache: A critical man, he was compactly built, brown-skinned and had a bland, square face. He wore long, fine, straight, dark brown hair and had brown eyes. A hunter by nature, he particularly liked to hunt and kill people for sport. He was simply known as **Necroshock.**

Charles Dalison: This cold-hearted, gregarious, former college professor was ivory skinned with bright blue eyes, and black hair. He was fragile to some degree, with a thin, sharp-featured face. Incarcerated for assisting multiple suicides, it was never proven that all of the deaths were voluntary. He was called **Gravebone.**

Giles Marshall: An analytical genius who was always quiet, he was a slight man with a craggy face and had long brown hair, grey-green eyes and tan skin. No one ever knew why he went to prison, only that he spent a considerable amount of time in psychiatric care. They called him **Hornsoak.**

Matthew Taylor: a muscular man with long, silky strawberry blond hair. He was a brave soul with an interest in plants. He was married, with several children until he killed them all. He was known as **Venomspawn.** (This was the deacon Matthew that Richard had spoken to for directions.)

Stephen Vaughan: small with a thin, jagged face, he had coarse, curly brown hair and grey-green eyes. At one time he was a coppersmith who was gentle by nature, and undemonstrative. He was in prison for plotting to blow up a local government building. He was called **Evilvenom**.

Thomas Benett: a fat man with fair hair, bright blue eyes, no eyebrows and a long, mournful face. He was once married, with several children and from all outward appearances seemed happy. He had no recollection of any of them now. They went missing and were never found. He was the prime suspect in their disappearance. However, with nothing more than an assumption, proving guilt was difficult, and so it was never to be. He was known as **Oceansludge.**

This group of men, assembled with one leader known as Preacher encompassed the earliest members of The Circle.

They never spoke to any of the citizen of Jesusland in a casual manner; they spoke only to Preacher and surrounded him constantly. No one got to Preacher without first getting past The Circle.

Then there were the drugs; Valium, Quaaludes, stimulants, barbiturates, opium, morphine, and LSD. Rumors spread wildly about Preacher's health as a result of this, and everyone remained concerned that some among them would fall victim to death by overdose. Most chose a careful approach to Preacher.

The bible study/prayer meeting as it was called, was little more than the ranting of a madman dressed in Christian clothing, all in the name of God. These were typically long winded speeches that were a litany of hand selected Bible verses chosen with the intention of supporting Preacher's anarchist theme. Although they rarely went over an hour or two, there were times depending on his mood, when they would go on until three or four in the morning. No one was allowed to leave, even to go to the bathroom so it was not unusual for several of the faithful to relieve themselves on the worship room floor.

Jesusland was nothing more than a concentration camp; a prison without walls or fences. So, why did people stay? Surely en mass they could have left? One on one, Preacher was very charming, friendly, warm, and loving. He fathered dozens of children during his 3 years at Jesusland. Most of the women in the commune would freely submit to him at his whim. It was similar to the Stockholm syndrome which over time creates a reverse effect during hostage taking, the victim becomes a willing supporter of the offender. Preacher had amazing mind control properties, was able to get anyone to do things he wanted, and used it every chance he got. In this case, it paralyzed almost 50 lost souls.

6 months later…

At the sound of the evening worship bells ringing, all of the citizens of Jesusland filed methodically into the large Worship hall known as the Citadel of the Altar of God. The worship hall rose to a height of 328 feet which included a 57 foot cross, and contained many bells, each one weighing almost a ton. The view of the Hills of the Heroic Past was amazing and wonderful. The crowd grew quiet as Preacher approached the podium. Silence abounded as he opened his Bible and began the sermon:

"Where is the Lord, and in what place shall we find Him? When the end comes how will we know that He has come for us?

The 18 hour or 9/3rds Day clock is purported evil against humanity in support of salvation—indicting every human on Earth as uneducated, and a waste of time in Gods' eyes.

For imagine a 3 sided Earth that has 3 days within a single day as we know it today. And as Humans evolve from Children, children belong to God. The empire WILL destroy us unless we destroy it first. He who has ears let him hear.

This is an issue of major importance to us now. You must hear this message and hear all that it implies. "

He paused momentarily, took a sip of water, and left the podium to continue the sermon in the midst of the congregation. His actions and bodily motions were jerky and irrational and as his voice grew louder the pace grew more intense. He acted like a madman…he continued

Isaiah 55:1(NIV)

1 "Come, all you who are thirsty, come to the waters; and you who have no money,

come, buy and eat! Come, buy wine and milk without money and without cost."

Revelation 1:4-6 (NIV)

3Blessed is the one who reads the words of this prophecy, and blessed are those who hear it and take to heart what is written in it, because the time is near.

…And from the seven spirits before his throne, and from Jesus Christ, who is the faithful witness, the firstborn from the dead, and the ruler of the kings of the earth.

To him who loves us and has freed us from our sins by his blood, and has made us to be a kingdom and priests to serve his God and Father—to him be glory and power forever and ever! Amen. "

I am the one who reads the words of this prophecy; you are the ones one who read the words of this prophecy; because the time is near.

In fact the time is so much closer than you think. I can be your salvation, and you can all become like me, like God."

"Wait!" Richard stood as he interrupted the sermon. "That's enough. It is described in Genesis 5 "For God knows that when you eat of it your eyes will be opened, and you will be like God, knowing good and evil." is this not the Serpent in the garden speaking? Is this not Satan himself?"

An hush came over the crowd and all eyes were on Richard. Just as quickly, the focus of their attention returned to Preacher, whose face had began to turn varying shades of red.

"Excellent point, Mr. Tinsley" Preacher shouted with renewed enthusiasm. "Please allow me to clarify…". In saying so, the seven demons in The Circle stood in anticipation of an altercation. Preacher raised his hand open palmed, as if to calm everyone down, but it was actually a gesture intended for The Circle.

"What I meant to say was," he started with calm in his voice. "That the knowledge of Faith is from God and..."

"You are not my salvation, Preacher." Richard interrupted. "You will never be my salvation. Jesus is my only salvation, and you are not The Messiah as you claim! I am appalled that all of you so calmly believe this to be the Word of God, when it is little more than a sham. We will have nothing further to do with it! We're leaving, and I suggest that you all do the same while you can." And with that Richard and Mary left abruptly, while Preacher continued his rant, as if nothing had changed. But of course it had. Upon their leaving, the massive worship hall doors, constructed from a heavy dark brown teakwood, crashed shut with a thud, and securely locked themselves. The floor to ceiling stained glass windows, adorned with red velvet curtains, one by one were drawn closed by an invisible hand. At the same time, a massive crack occurred in the wall behind the cross. "This night", Preacher said sadly with a tremble to his voice while staring downward at the floor. "It is lost."

Still early in the evening, Richard and Mary went back to their cabin. Richard insisted that Mary go ahead of him into Caperville and get a room for the night at the local hotel and he would join her later. He gave very clear instructions that if he could not get to her by morning she was to take the bus back to Jeff City. He would meet her there in a few days. Reluctantly, she did as he asked.

They walked out of the compound, hand in hand down the mountain and onto the main road. It was only few moments before the bus pulled up. He kissed her goodbye as if he somehow knew it would be the last time he would ever see her, and then watched solemnly as the old city bus pulled away and drove out of sight, leaving a familiar cloud of dust.

From a cloud of dust to darkness of night and to then to eventual dawn, Mary Tinsley found herself in Caperville at The Wagon Wheel Motel unable to sleep, waiting for Richard. But like his father before him, he never arrived. So, with much trepidation she called the police to report him missing.

The FBI had been watching the Jesusland compound for several years as a result of the so-called accidents. To date, none of the investigations had lead to arrests. The investigations had all been closed. Each of the autopsies had supported the claim of accidental deaths, save one deemed a suicide. And as with all of the previous, this morning would be no different.

Jesusland had become an apocalyptic cult that was especially dangerous because it was biblically based. Preacher and his followers viewed the millennium as the time that signals a major world transformation. They believed that the battle against Satan, as detailed in the Book of Revelation, would begin in the years surrounding the millennium and that the federal government would be an arm of Satan. Therefore, they believed the millennium would bring about a battle between cult members — religious martyrs —and the government, and if they did not act then they would fall victim to certain demise.

As a cult, Jesusland was composed of individuals who demonstrated great devotion to a person and a movement all in the name of God. However, using that definition, Jesusland was actually a domestic terrorist group characterized as *Christian Identity-like* cults. That's how the FBI and the DEA saw it, which is why they elected to watch that group. In the scope of their world and their thinking, a cult like Jesusland followed a belief that the main Spiritual leader had some special talent, gift, or knowledge that would ultimately deliver the group from darkness to Heaven. That definition of cults provided important distinctions that were vital in analyzing the cult's fondness for violence, as they saw it.

The morning sun crept over the rolling hills of San Sabena County and reflected its' brightness through the light haze. Off in the distance, a convoy of black Lincoln Continentals, complete with blackout tinted windows and bullet proofing panels, moved towards Jesusland with precision, speed, and purpose. One by one the government vehicles made the slight left turn from the main road to the mountain and onto the entrance of Jesusland. There were several sheriff deputy cars already there, emergency lights twirling, flashing in and out of unison.

The lead investigator was a man named Travis. He was the first one to notice that while standing at the entrance to the Worship Hall there was music echoing from inside the Hall. He stood quietly listening with his head slightly angled, one fist partially clenched and the other on his holstered .44 Magnum; he slowly reached for the door. As it opened he was met with an unforgettable sight and sound.

A wave of stench; a horrible smell was the first thing that greeted Travis as it poured out of the first available exit. It was the music that next struck Travis. As if on cue; it was piped through the PA system and was loud enough to drown out any conversations. The remaining team of FBI agents, donned in full SWAT apparel, filed quickly in and out of the facility to the music of *Funny* by the Albert Pion Quartet…

Funny…I practiced every day,
To find some clever lines to say,
To make the meaning come through...
I get on with life as a dreamer,
I'm a funny kinda person that way.

The 48 remaining members of Jesusland, people seeking the truth in an ever ugly world, were all dead. They apparently died in a carefully orchestrated suicide that involved barbiturates and other drugs. All of the victims; men, women, and children believed that they had been chosen to go to Heaven and that the previous night was the time do so. They were no signs of a struggle; no bloodshed or defensive wounds. No indications that the victims were strangled; no bruises, no ligature marks on the neck or bleeding in the throat. No fracture of the hyoid bone or evidence of petechial hemorrhages—the tiny red spots in the eyes. The crime scene was very clean.

The mass suicide was accomplished by intravenous ingestion. First, sodium pentothal, a fast-acting barbiturate was administered; second, pancuronium bromide, a chemical paralytic agent; and third, potassium chloride, a compound that caused cardiac arrest. All died as the result of the lethal drug cocktail. This would be a precursor to the state sponsored lethal injection used in executions.

All of the collapsible chairs had been folded, stacked, and neatly put in their place. The 48 members of the cult were found lying neatly in rows of 8 on the floor. All were dressed in identical black velvet robes embroidered with stars and a green and white peace symbol button on the left front crest. The sleeves were voluminous and the flared openings were adorned with black lace. All of the victims were barefoot and wearing sunglasses. They held identical crosses in their left hand and identical Bibles in the other. Obviously, they did not die all at one time and no doubt they ingested the lethal cocktail one group at a time, so as to retain the orderliness they left behind.

I get on with life as a dreamer,
I'm a funny kinda person that way.

I'm not so fond of loneliness,
I just think back to you,
And I'm happy once again.

Travis made his way through the crowd of devotees until he found the source of the music; a tape player on a continuous loop, and turned it off. Next to it there was an envelope; on the front was written, "From: The Sevenfold Spirit", while on the back was written: "For Travis"

Of course, he promptly opened it and began to read:

Travis—you do not know me. I am not of this world, but I come to you as a messenger of The Lord. I have only a short amount of time—so I must tell you this quickly, and do so under cover of this would-be suicide note.

What you are witnessing here in this place, is the work of evil, Orchestrated by the Prince of Darkness himself. It will not stop here. Many more will die in his name, and it will culminate over the next 30 years. They will be called Church Assassins and they will attempt to bring down the Faithful, but they will not succeed. However, their number will continue to grow, and they will try..

There is one person that you must find before they do. Mary Tinsley is one of two surviving members of this group. She left here last night—she will soon have a child. This child will be greatly sought after as she will have supernatural abilities given to her by God to do His work and she will possess a special gift as a result. Once she gains an understanding of what these gifts mean, she will unknowingly expose the evil one for exactly what he is, inadvertently turning the unbelieving world from *their* cause towards the Love of Our God through Jesus Christ. The Dark Prince will not rest until he finds her and destroys her, as risking exposure of his world would not be acceptable.

The other surviving member of this cult is a man called Preacher. You would do well to remember his name, as an unexpected encounter with this individual would be most unfortunate.

With your God given skills, you are the only one capable of finding Mary Tinsley's daughter— I implore you to do so and do so quickly. The Dark One will not rest, and neither should you.

May the God of Peace be with you through all of your days, and that your daily walk with Jesus is as profound as ever. Amen.

As one of his fellow agents walked by, he nonchalantly folded the letter and slipped it in his pocket. After a few moments, he looked at it again and amazing enough, the contents of the angelic letter were gone; the ink had disappeared entirely and there was no trace of it at all. He flipped it over to check out the reverse side thinking he had it backwards, but no such luck. The message, like the messenger, had vanished.

He was W. Rodger Travis, but everyone just called him Travis. He was a lean man with a craggy face. He had long, wavy, dark brown hair and brown eyes. A sullen loner, he was fanatical by nature and could be judgmental but when it served his purposes he was witty and charismatic. He was also a soldier…a self made mercenary.

Shortly after Travis graduated from East Rivertree University in Rivertree, Indiana he was unsure what to do with his life. Bored and directionless he sat in his small all-purpose box of a studio apartment staring out the window at the raging blizzard that brewed outside. While waiting for a break in the bad weather, he got a call from his friend Randy. Their mutual friend Matt had invited them to come to San Francisco for a few weeks. It didn't take long for Travis to decide to go. Much to the chagrin of his aunt and uncle, the next day Travis and Randy were on the road from Rivertree to San Francisco. Enamored with all that the city had to offer, the Golden Gate Bridge, Alcatraz, Sausalito, Pacific coast and the Wine country, Travis knew there would be no returning to the Midwest.

Matt, Randy, and Travis took the trolley down to the Harbor View Tavern. They laughed, had far too much drink and otherwise had a really great time! Randy came from a very wealthy family and gave little thought or concern as to money and where it might come from—it was a foregone conclusion that he would always be wealthy. In fact, the years to come would bear this out when his parents passed away they left him millions. Matt was an intern at San Francisco Medical University diligently pursuing his doctorate in psychology, and had long ago been given the handle of "Doc" by his friends.

Afterward, they went back to Matt's apartment and barbecued ribs and chicken, but before the sun set they had time to walk to

Half Moon Bay. Unfortunately, they were very hurried to get back to the apartment and didn't get to see much. They were already making plans for the next outing.

After a few weeks, Travis got a job, actually 2 jobs, neither of which had anything at all to do with his major. He started selling used cars, never believing that he had any selling skills, yet in quite a short period of time did very well. At night he was a bouncer at Wild Parrots; a discotheque located in Haight-Ashbury.

About six months later, he moved from San Francisco to Los Angeles and lived in Lake Bayhurst. Life in Southern California was fun, at least until he ran out of money and the time came to concentrate on finding a job in his college major.

Travis had always wanted to be a cop. Nothing more really, so he decided to follow his dream. His first job was in narcotics with the Redvale Police Department as a junior detective. From there he applied for and was accepted into the FBI and after graduating from the academy he began his career as an undercover narcotics agent.

His first assignment lasted 28 months. He was given the task of infiltrating the notorious "D-Posse" which was a dangerous motorcycle gang that traveled predominantly in the desert southwest and Mexico. Sporting shoulder length hair, an eye patch and a new name (Jack), Travis was soon accepted into the gang and began to climb the organizational ladder. Every step was a challenge and at every turn he was tested. He became so focused on his mission that he abandoned everything of importance to him; family, children, and a normal life as he knew it.

Although successful in obtaining the arrests of many in the gun and drug trade, he paid a terrible price for it. He lost everything, had numerous attempts on his life, and his house was torched by arsons. So at 36 years old, he returned to his home in California where he quietly ran the San Sabena County field office for the FBI. Quietly that is, until the night of the mass suicide at Jesusland.

Intently, his eyes scanned the makeshift morgue for something amiss in the organized chaos. Travis quickly realized from the body count that two were missing.

Travis walked out of the worship hall, stepped into a dark courtyard of sorts. As he lit a cigarette, his watchful eye scanned the area for any peculiarities. The crunch of pea gravel beneath his shoes was the only noticeable sound, when he stopped to pan the area. Turning slowly, he found himself staring at a massive cross and hanging from it, some 25 feet above the courtyard, was the battered body of Richard Tinsley. His hands and feet bound to the cross, a canvas restraint placed over his head. He was hung in such a way as to mimic The Crucifixion.

As they brought the body down, there was little doubt he was dead. From all appearances there had been a terrible struggle and it appeared to have been equitable in strength and ferocity. Like two pugilists in a twelve round match, a draw in which there is only a technical winner, both were exhausted; both were finished. However, clearly this was a battle Richard lost.

Apart from the severe bruising and scratches, the cause of death was not obvious making it difficult to believe that a fight had ended his life. In fact, that is exactly what happened. In the weeks ahead, the San Sabena County Coroner would rule the death resulted from "natural causes."

Travis stood at the entrance to the Worship Hall overlooking the courtyard. He was perplexed by all of it, and wondered if it could at all be connected to his own sordid past and undercover work. He knew the letter that was left for him was real, and believed it to be from God. He knew he had to find Mary Tinsley, he just did not know where to find her, why he needed to, or even what he would say to her once he found her.

At roughly the same time, a cross country bus was making its way back to Jeff City. Lulled to sleep by the drone of the vehicle, Mary Tinsley was on board. At one point she woke as the bus came to a stop. The doors opened with a swish and a small elderly lady slowly made her way up the steps and toward the back of the nearly full bus. Each step was purposeful and sure, but slow nonetheless, as the tedious task of putting one foot in front of the other continued. She was a fair-skinned woman with long, fine, straight white hair, blue-grey eyes and a heart-shaped face. She had a love of birds, especially cardinals and preferred the company of animals to that of people.

She stopped at the open seat next to Mary and asked if it was taken. Mary happily offered it to her. As she sat, she sighed heavily, relieved that the arduous task of walking was complete—at least for now. She turned to Mary with a crooked smile.

'What if God gave up on us?' She started. "Has He ever given up on you, dear? There is this idea that has shown up in some Christian circles that one's fate in the afterlife depends on the state of one's soul at the moment of death—so the sinful man who truly repents on his deathbed, eventually ends up in heaven.

I wonder if anyone has ever written a science fiction story about this? Imagine, for instance, that we can emulate a person in a television and can transmit people from one place to another. But the emulation isn't perfect—it emulates the person as he is when transmitted but much is lost in the process.

When you die, you are transmitted. If you happen to die angry, your image or continuation is an angry person—forever. On the other hand, if you die in a mood of repentance for your sins, your continuation is the person that you were at that moment. Interesting, don't you think?

I used to live in a town called Cardiff Grove; a small, curiously empty city at the edge of a desert which was best known as the birthplace of a John Cardiff Williamson, a famous hero in The Egyptian-Melanesian War. The majority of its citizens were involved in the community and it was considered noteworthy for its exceptionally pure water.

The house I lived in was small and well placed in a heavily wooded area near a creek. It was only two bedrooms, actually more a cottage than a house. The entry floor was a cold flagstone. I liked the way it felt. The walls were soft amber with a border of blue along the bottom. There was always a faint mustiness as you entered, but it dissipated with a surprising blast of air from the open door. The living area was a splendid room with dark green curtains that danced in the draft, the floor was a plush tan carpet and the walls were an ornate brick pattern. Our bedroom had a saw-dusty smell that was always evident. The flooring was a pattern of tiling, while the walls were haphazardly painted with white. How I used to love that room most.

I was married then—we had a little girl who was 2 years old when she died. How I miss her so, even today, all these years later. I was careless and should have paid greater attention. I know you will take good care of your child...I am so happy for you Dear...I know you'll make a wonderful Mother..."

Mary suddenly awoke, her eyes popping open with a start, as the bus hit a pothole in the road. She began mumbling something about not yet having children, and once fully awake realized that the elderly woman was gone. Actually, she was never there to begin with. It was all a dream.

The bus roared along the highway as if it owned the road, noisily making its' way down Route 66. With any luck at all, she would make the long trip from California to Jeff City in three days. She was devastated at the thought of having left behind her loving husband whom she feared was dead, but was ready to forget the awful memories of Jesusland.

6. Church Assassin

Pinewood Meadows—2006

On a frigid December morning, the untouched snow was clean and glistening white as the sun began to peak over the horizon again a cloudless sky. Acting as an acoustic blanket, everything was very still and quiet to an almost disturbing point.

Pinewood Meadows was a small town. Of the 1500 people who called it home, most of them worked the farms that had been in their families for hundreds of years. This fairly conservative city was located in the heart of the county seat and was considered noteworthy for it's abundance of garlic and sage. Small and peculiar in nature, it sat beside the river and was best known as a 'hellhole', by most of teenagers. Apart from school, church, and work there was little else to do in Pinewood Meadows. Like other communities, big or small, the majority of its families were quite involved with all of them.

The main street in Pinewood Meadows was actually State highway 132. As one entered the outskirts of town, State Highway 132 became Main Street. Albeit for only a 2 mile stretch, travel slowed from a comfortable 70 mph to an excruciatingly slow 25 mph. Waiting for each of those travelers was the local Sherriff, armed with radar gun in hand.

The town square, long since abandoned by any retailer worthy of being called an anchor had turned into an ideal location for antique shopping, grabbing a bite to eat at the hot dog stand, or just lounging on a park bench on a sunny day. Pioneer Meadows took pride in its impressive historic storefronts which lined the streets of the town square. As a testament, a walk through the doors of the stately structures easily conjured up images of an attractive by-gone age. For example The Altman Block Building (1892), on the corner of Stark and Main Streets, stood as one of the most prominent and ornate structures on the town square. The Squire Temple, as majestic as ever, stood in its original glory with very little work done to it apart from maintenance. Finally, the old Pioneer County Criminal Court Building now played host to a restaurant featuring Al Capone memorabilia. Just past the town square, Main Street was lined with tidy homes reminiscent of the turn of the century. Many were small but quaint with their picket fences, clapboard siding and neatly manicured lawns. Others were quite remarkable. The historic gable-end gothic revival was trimmed in clapboard and sported a variety of window treatments. It was believed to have been built in 1858, but courthouse records listed it as 1879. The Stryker family lived there for 55 years. Mr. Stryker was the first school teacher in St. Joseph, the nearest adjacent town at the time. He rode his horse there each day. Stryker Middle School in Willoughby was named after this early educator. The exterior woodwork, the various window arches, the carriage step at the curb and surviving horse ring made it a notable homestead. One of the oldest surviving homes in Pioneer County was built in 1847 by Wilfred S. Covington. Covington arrived in Pioneer Meadows during the 1830's from the east Coast. Covington Street is named after this early family.

From Main Street there was a gravel road that went under the S&O train trestle. Just off the road sat the church. At first appearances, it was unassuming and cold and simply nothing more than an all white clapboard building. However, on closer inspection, it was apparent that it was much more than that. The building really was an antique, built sometime in the 1850's. The steps leading to the double doors had been replaced many times, but the Newell posts appeared original and creaked when used. Just past the large oak double door was a short foyer, followed by rows of hand hewn benches on either side of the main aisle. The floors were also constructed of old oak planks in varying sizes and thicknesses, and the walls were painted a drab white. Typically, a languid wind came through the open windows on the west side of the building—stirring the institutional-like grey curtains. It was a simple, sparsely decorated room with a few scattered pictures. But its greatest attribute was a wash of sunlight, reflecting warmth from one wall to the next, throughout the rather high-ceilinged facility. At the front of the worship hall was a single podium, a relatively large wooden cross hanging behind it, and two unremarkable floor candelabras. There were no risers for the choir. Not that singing was banned, but rather it was believed to be unnecessary and was not a part of that particular church's creed.

The sign in the front of the Gladdish church read "Pioneer Meadows Church—All are welcome".

Indeed all were.

Pioneer Meadows Church met for regular worship, every weekend, without fail. They worshipped the Sabbath, in the traditional sense, so Saturday rather than Sunday became their focused day with God. Certain early Gladdish traditions called for Sunday service, but over time this was altered and somehow just stuck. The Gladdish Church organization met annually in Europe, Asia, Africa, and parts of the U.S.

The worship doctrine, or sermon was usually unscripted. As a religion based in silence, the pulpit was typically available to whoever felt "moved by the Spirit to speak". This allowed any individual in the congregation to minister for as long as they felt it was right. There was no "bonafide leader" in such a service. The Gladdish worshipped in this tradition and believed that each person is equal before God and is capable of knowing "the light" or the Holy Spirit, directly. Over time, very few remaining churches managed to sustain the unscripted style of worship and until recently Pioneer Meadows was one of those. Most of the surviving Gladdish churches offered a prepared message, more in touch with mainstream Christianity and it was delivered by an individual with some theological training. In this more forward Gladdish movement there was a sermon, Bible readings and prayer, hymns and silent worship. Often there was a paid pastor responsible for the care of the members of the local church. This kind of Gladdish church represented the vast majority of their membership who were evangelical and had parted from the unscripted worship of old.

The Gladdish had no creed but always had doctrines. More in touch with actions in accordance to the leading of the Spirit, The Fathers of the Gladdish (the would-be Deacons of the church), historically had a greater desire for understanding coming from God's Spirit than the notions of theology. Rather than acquiesce to the leaders of the day as the authoritative principle regarding God, they chose their own way of seeking His authority by aligning themselves with the foundation that they would be lead by the Holy Spirit.

The Gladdish seemed unusual because of their emphasis on a personal experience with God. As a result, they become to be known throughout the years as a Mystic Religion. However, it differed from other mystical religions in at least two important ways. For one, Gladdish mysticism was a group centered effort rather than focused on a specific individual, and as such it would be conceivable that the unscripted meeting for worship was considered an expression of that group. Everyone listened together for the Spirit of God to move them and anyone may be called to say something on their heart. Similar to a monastic sect, they quietly lived a mystic life and tradition throughout the years. They simply chose not to withdraw from the organized world of Christianity, but rather elected to translate mysticism into action. In doing so, the actions became the foundation of their religion evidenced by the moving of the Spirit of God unto them. Although many criticized them as mere humanists, it was obvious that they were able to be led by the Holy Spirit; moved to speak not in tongues, without ranting and rambling sermons, or epileptic gyrations or motions; but simple unscripted devotion to God through the Holy Spirit, as they supposed it to be.

At sunrise, on a cold Sunday morning in the midwestern prairie, flat for as far as the eye could see; there was no one around as the little sleepy eyed town began to stir. The heater vents and chimneys of the houses emitted puffy white smoke into a cloudless blue sky and in an unorganized and chaotic manner, one by one the inhabitants began to stir and ready themselves for the day.

It was not unusual that the parking lot of the Pioneer Meadows Church had only one car in it from the previous night's service; but it was remarkable that it was the one belonging to the Pastor. It remained untouched from the Saturday Worship service, evidenced by the covering of ice and snow that glistened in morning sunlight.

The coffee pot moaned and groaned, hissing steam in a frantic manner as it struggled to evaporate the last drop of water in its' reservoir. For just a moment, it settled down a bit and all seemed well until Travis grabbed the pot by the handle and began to pour a cup. He replaced it somewhat awkwardly and the coffee proceeded to drip onto the hot burner and the frenetic hissing sound and the smell of burning coffee resumed.

His office was as one might expect; after all, he said his attention was focused on catching the bad guys, not in filing or organizing paperwork. And it showed. It was a mess, albeit tidy, a mess that made little or no sense to anyone on the outside looking in. There were stacks of files, papers, magazines, etc., abundant enough to cover the entire top of the desk. But Travis knew *what* was there, *where* it was, and *how* to find what he was looking for. He had little trouble with his filing system and really didn't care if anyone had a problem with it.

Life had been particularly hard on Travis since the Massacre at Jesusland, and it showed. His long dark brown hair had since gone gray, and was considerably shorter; he walked with a profound limp as a result of a fall from a second story rooftop while in pursuit of a bank robber; he had re-married and divorced again, and tried in vain, sadly, to have some kind of relationship with his children.

Not everything was bad though; he was awarded the FBI Star, the FBI Medal for Meritorious Achievement 5 times to date; he also had made several promotions, but the most meaningful was the position of Section Chief for Domestic Terrorism Unit. The primary purpose of his new job was to address the challenges of emerging national security and criminal threats. This promotion occurred after the murder of Rev. Seth Davidson, the brother of Senator Jack Davidson. The Senator learned of the details of the murder and the commitment that Travis had to solving this case and the senator pushed vigorously for the promotion. In this new position, Travis was dedicated to a national intelligence workforce and had authority through embedded intelligence elements in each FBI Headquarters division and in the Bureau's field offices.

He was required to relocate from San Francisco to St. Louis and after The Massacre at Jesusland he was happy to do so.

With coffee in one hand, he pulled the half broken chair out from the desk, sat down, and began the day. In one of the many neat piles was a stack of folders, maybe a dozen or more. There were all the same: they had the initials *CA* and the words *Classified* stamped in bright red ink with a month and year written in the upper right hand corner. In the tab portion of the manila folder there was a name of a person and of a city.

CA stood for *Church Assassin* and it was the only case he had really worked for more than 30 years. As was his routine each day (including weekends) he came to the office, got a cup of coffee and began to read each file. He did this meticulously to insure that he never missed a single detail, but was always sure he had. Since the mass murder/suicide at Jesusland some years earlier, many things had changed, including Travis. The Messenger of The Lord who spoke to him that fateful night warned that there would be many more, and needless to say there were. The unsolved case would become the longest reigning serial killer case in U.S. history. However, history would not recognize it, not yet anyway, because it had been kept a well guarded secret for all those years. Travis and the FBI had become adept at spinning it to the news media so that they would be diverted toward the next newsworthy story. The serial killer called *Church Assassin* would remain a largely unpublicized mystery for many years.

The murders did not begin right away after the Jesusland Massacre. It would be many years later and in an obscure part of the country. Almost always at night and always in a church, for more than 30 years the Church Assassin had managed an average of 2 or 3 killings a year. They all displayed very similar, now familiar traits: the inside of the church worship hall was neat, tidy and relatively undisturbed; the bodies were well dressed in a purple sermon robe and hung from a large alter cross on the wall; all were either shot execution style in the back of the head, beaten to death, or strangled. There were never any witnesses; the scene had been well cleaned including blood, shell casings, bullets, trace evidence, etc.. The office of the church was typically ransacked as if the serial killer was looking for something or someone, and it was always left in a terrific mess. The murders that followed Jesusland (60 plus in all) were flawlessly executed and went undetected; except one—the one that led to Preachers arrest.

Travis reached for the top file, the Jesusland Massacre. He flipped through the notes and loose papers, various forms and remarks. He had examined it so many times before, but he always looked with the same intensity as if it were the first time. With one hand he pulled out a cigarette, stuck it in his mouth and lit it, while flipping through the pages with the other. The Polaroid's from 30 years previous, though worn and faded with time bore out the painful memory of Preacher and his evil work.

Travis had long since determined that the murders came in surges in terms of number and location. The first surge was located on the West Coast, while the second did not begin until much later and was located in the Colorado and Montana areas. The trail would go cold, and then out of nowhere it would start all over again. So it was, Preacher resumed killing in September, a year and a half later and it started with the murder of Josh Witherspoon, who was just the beginning. He strangled the young man, covering his face with his trademark canvas restraint mask and hung the body from the cross on the outside of the building. It was in a relatively rural setting with the cross side of the building obscured from direct sight so it took days for anyone to find it. Preacher ended the month by killing Pastor Michael Johns, a fifty-six year old from Longtown, Colorado. He was found in the same way; hanging from the alter cross, badly beaten with the canvas restraint mask over his head, dead.

A month later on Halloween, he made a critical mistake. His victim was Rev. Cyril Wright. Preacher did not know that as result of far too many burglaries, the Church was armed with micro wired, pinhole closed circuit TVs, and that they were running at the time Preacher committed his murderous act.

Rev. Wright was found only a few hours later and when the local police arrived, the detectives on the scene had a chance to view the tapes. It was all there in its entirety; the police could finally put a face to this heinous killer and they set out to find him.

Travis knew that all serial killers no matter their reasoning or religious beliefs, possessed very similar character traits. He was aware that most were white males between 25 and 35 years old; that they were of either high or low income; possessed average to high intelligence, and were usually married with children.

As a matter of profile etiquette, he also knew that many serial killers had a history of physical and/or sexual abuse during childhood, that in nearly half of them the biological father had left before the child was 12 years old, and acts like pyromania, theft, and animal cruelty were all shared traits.

Furthermore, he knew that Serial killers enjoyed prolonging the victims suffering and pain and that they played God in determining when a victim would die. As such, it might not be unusual for them to torture their victim for days at a time in order to obtain the greatest pleasure possible. In contrast however, the victims typically had no profile and were chosen at random; the result of being in the wrong place at the wrong time. Preacher had a very specific victim profile. In this case, his stated victim had more to do with God than with being a Pastor. It was important that Preacher chose the right place and that it had the right setting and props; namely a robust alter cross, and his trademark canvas restraint masks that were donned by all of his victims. Using a prop like the canvas restraint mask humiliated the victim with depraved specificity, in a symbolic attempt to humiliate God as well.

Travis later learned that Preacher chose to do this to create anonymity, much in the way an executioner in past time would have done. Only in his case it was the victims who were hooded, not the criminally condemned.

The next day Travis arrived and assumed control of the investigation.

About a week later, they got a tip that would change everything; a fax came into the Billings FBI field office that brought welcomed news:

RE: BILLINGS MONTANA TO BUREAU.

MOUNTAIN CABIN, LOCATED APPROX 6 MILES FROM TOWN OF CROWNEPOINT BELIEVED TO BE BROKEN INTO AND OCCASIONALLY OCCUPIED. CABIN BREAK—IN REPORTED BY CARETAKER; SUBJECT IS CONSIDERED ARMED AND EXTREMELY DANGEROUS. ESCAPE RISK.

And so it was, that would become the day the Church Assassin would be apprehended. They found Lucas Pritchard asleep on the sofa in the abandoned cabin.

However, it was a victory that would be short lived. Once incarcerated in the county jail, he had somehow acquired a hacksaw blade, probably from another prison inmate. Each night he slowly and carefully sawed through a small metal plate in the ceiling. After a near starvation diet he was able to fit through the hole and the crawl space above. So, on the night of December 24, 1974, he packed clothes and books under his blanket to make it look like he was sleeping. Squeezing through the hole in the ceiling, he crawled to the place just above an interior bathroom, dropped down into it, and walked out the front door undetected.

Preacher was free. He ran a half a mile along Sutton Street, the main drag in town and escaped into the hills south of town. A short time later he hitched a ride into Billings, boarded a plane bound for Indianapolis, and caught a bus to St. Louis.

By the time anyone realized he had escaped, Preacher was long gone.

Travis grabbed the folder; the top one marked Crownepoint 1974, and opened to the profile sheet…

For most people the day had not yet begun, especially given that it was a Sunday. For Travis, there would be no rest; no vacation, no stopping or slowing down the investigation; no giving in; no quitting of any kind, no matter what day of the week it was. With all of the challenges of the case and sleep being in short supply, the quiet of Sunday mornings was his time to rejuvenate. But all of that was shattered in an instant when the phone rang, breaking whatever concentration he had.

He listened intently as police in the small farming community told him they were on high alert after a local pastor had been brutally beaten while awaiting parishioners in her church. Upon entry, they had found the badly mutilated body of Mary Richards, 68, in Pioneer Meadows Church. They went on to say that they thought Richards's body had been "staged," meaning it was moved into an unnatural position. Travis inquired about the reference to the 'unnatural position' and asked that they elaborate more; they responded saying she was hung from the altar cross in a position resembling the crucifixion. Furthermore, they had not yet determined whether that church had been specifically targeted, and were open to any and all support they could get. Surveillance video had shown her car arriving at the church about 10 a.m. Saturday but nothing further had been detected. They knew only a few things for certain: a visitor who arrived at the church shortly before noon saw Richards's car but found the door to the church locked; a retired pastor and his son arrived at the church shortly after noon that day and they saw Richards' car parked at the church, but when they were unable to get into the building, they became concerned and called police, he said.

The police entered the church, and found Richards' body. They discouraged the Pastor and his son from going inside because of the condition and placement of the body which had been severely beaten.

The once-peaceful congregation at the little white church in the pristine town had been rocked to its' core. Even those who did not belong to the church or any church for that matter were shaken by the event.

Events of that magnitude, of that proportion, never happened there. Pioneer Meadows would never be the same.

So, there it was; it had happened yet again. Travis would hear a familiar routine with contempt, yet he listened intently to the law officer on the other end of the line as if that was the first call, the first murder, or the first church. He scribbled some notes on a yellow pad, here and there, not in any particular order, and no doubt no one other than Travis would be able to decipher them. He asked a few questions and shortly thereafter hung up the phone.

Within a few hours he arrived in Pine Meadows, and began an investigation into what would become the 61st murder by the Church Assassin; some 34 years after the Jesusland Massacre. However, this time would be different as it would provide the greatest insight into the mind of a depraved and psychopathic killer, and the greatest lead as to motive.

When Travis arrived the perimeter had already been cordoned off with the familiar yellow tape; another crime scene destined to hold the same circumstances, lack of evidence and reason. However, the circumstances surrounding this event were different from any of the previous. Without realizing it, Travis was about to get very lucky.

He flashed his badge and FBI credentials at the state trooper standing at the front of the church and opened the door to a familiar sound…

…Funny, I'm not so fond of loneliness,
I just think back to you,
And I'm happy once again.
I'm a funny kinda person that way.

"Turn that thing damn off!" he barked at the State Trooper, who quickly did as instructed. He reached for the lights and flipped them all on; throwing light from floods and spots that cast such a surreal illumination. The scene was similar, yet notably different. One spotlight in particular cast a subtle light on the alter cross that was hanging on the wall just behind the podium. Travis walked purposefully toward the cross, carefully eyeing the surroundings for anything that might remotely resemble a clue. There was something different though, something scribbled above the cross. Although difficult to see at first, the closer he got the more clear it became. In just the right light, he saw it at last—written in blood above the cross was:

This is it…

He stood there expressionless, staring at the words, perplexed by the seeming riddle and its' meaning. He glanced toward the ground and noticed a scrap of paper. As he picked it up, to his surprise he realized it was a newspaper clipping. It was crumpled and torn in some places but it was still legible nonetheless.

St. Louis—It was announced that celebrated Child Psychologist Dr. Matthew Reiber will by the keynote speaker at the Psychotherapy and the Spiritual World Conference on on January 11, 2007 at the Belgium Cathedral.

Dr. Reiber is the founder of a breakthrough treatment for children previously diagnosed with autism spectrum disorders, such as Asperger's Syndrome. "Through Self Children" as he has termed them, employs the controversial use of thought transference or clairvoyance as a means of reaching and communicating with the child. The first patient, Sabra Torrington, 33, long cured of her previously diagnosed symptoms will be in attendance and will issue a brief statement commending the doctor's work.

At last, Travis knew something that Preacher did not. The Pastor's latest victim was not dead, but rather that she remained alive if just barely. The other thing that was obvious was that the newspaper clipping was left unintentionally. Finally, he knew where Preacher was going next, when he would be there. Travis didn't yet know why Preacher was headed there, but he would be sure to be there to greet him.

The Rev. Mary Clarisse Richards began her ministry by serving as an associate pastor at Northmont Gladdish Church and as minister of pastoral care at Ridgemont Community Church in nearby Brookston. She also served as chaplain at both the Pioneer Meadows Retirement Home and Community Memorial Hospital. For the past eighteen years, she trained chaplains at the University Medical Center in Columbia.

A native of Missouri, Richards graduated from Wycliffe School of Theology. Briefly married then widowed, she had only one child. Apart from that, no one really knew very much about her.

She never had issues with anyone, was adored by everyone, and considered to be a rock in the community. So when she had the opportunity to become the senior pastor of the Pioneer Meadows Gladdish Church, there was no question about her filling the position.

The Rev. Mary Richards proved to be an instant hit with the locals, and in the first month attendance at Sunday services rose by 30%. The introduction of Saturday evening worship was also wildly successful.

The Pioneer Meadows newspaper, *The Daily Reporter* interviewed her shortly after her appointment. Something she was initially uncomfortable with, but nonetheless she acquiesced. When asked about her opinion regarding the role of religion and science in today's ministry she replied:

"…When we separate the two, we are left with a very frightening scenario. This of course, is the scientist operating without any particular moral anchor, as well as that of the religious leader operating without any respect to scientific revelation. Independent of each other, they can do severe damage from a community point of view. There is a place for both—and it is imperative for religious leaders to recognize this and employ it in their teachings. Our intellects are gifts from God, precious gifts. Separating science from religion and religion from science impoverishes both, which does not serve God in the way He expects…"

Why such a morbid and tragic event had befallen such a humble servant of God was a mystery to Travis, but he was determined to continue the search until Preacher was caught. Travis had seen many things throughout his career, but nothing was more challenging than standing before the battered and badly beaten body of Pastor Richards. There would be no interview on this day.

Her eyes were swollen shut; they no longer looked like eyes at all, but rather like two large, dark purple bulbs; reminiscent of over ripened plums. Broken in several places, her nose was now almost completely flattened. Most of her teeth had been knocked out and her lips were bright blue and many times larger than normal. As if that were not enough, her jaw had been broken and had to be wired shut.

There was little or nothing that could be done at this point and any attempt at interviewing Pastor Richards would be futile. Although the University Medical Center had the finest trauma team in the state, they had done everything they could, and now it was in God's hands.

Travis closed the door behind him as he left her room. His heart was heavy with sorrow for this woman. As he left the ICU unit, a reporter from the local newspaper asked a nearby doctor about the pastors' condition. Making his way towards the elevators, he heard the attending physician reply that Reverend Mary Richards Tinsley had indeed passed away at 11:10 p.m. the result of injuries sustained by blunt force trauma.

7. The darkest place in the world St. Louis—The Belgium Cathedral

Sunday January 11, 2007—8:21 p.m.

...Upon hearing the explosion, knowing full well the nature of the concussion and the muffled reverberation it left in its' wake, Travis tossed his half smoked cigarette to the ground. He stepped from the foot path thru an opening in the trees and ran across the street to The Belgium Cathedral. Reaching into his back pocket for his radio and with one hand he called for everyone to move in, and with the other he pulled out the heavy .44 magnum from his shoulder holster. *Black Rainstorm* was in full effect.

Black Rainstorm was lead by an elite Special Operations division of the FBI. Well trained to perform high-risk operations outside the normal expectations of officers, they were known simply as TKO; Tactical Killing Operations. Training included hostage negotiations and extractions, serving extremely risky arrest and search warrants, apprehending barricaded suspects, and confronting profoundly well-armed criminals. The TKO team was outfitted with specialized firearms including assault rifles, submachine guns, pump riot shotguns, carbines, riot control agents, stun grenades, and high-powered rifles for use by snipers. In addition to their firepower, their specialized equipment included armored vehicles, entry and extraction tools, highly developed night vision apparatus, extreme body armor and motion detectors used for determining the location of hostages or criminals from the inside of an enclosed building.

TKO support included K9 Units, flash bang, stinger and tear gas grenades.

As was typical for their unit, they carried a wide variety of weapons in service. However, the semi-automatic pistol remained the most popular sidearm. They primarily used Glock's and Berettas, but weren't limited only to those; they also used common submachine guns which included a .9 mm and .10 mm. The shotguns used by the TKO unit included a semi automatic version. It was effective, precise and had a very manageable recoil system. The carbine tended to be the favored rifle because it afforded the team increased accuracy at longer ranges. The compact size of these weapons was essential as they were often forced to operate in a close quarter surroundings.

They had a variety of options that could be used to break down doors quickly; shotguns, explosive charges, or battering rams used to demolish the door frame or smash the lock or hinges. Their arsenal included less-deadly weapons well; shotguns loaded with bean bag rounds, tasers, pepper ball guns, pepper spray canisters, and other incapacitating agents.

If the term "lethal agent" was defined as intent to kill, then a non-lethal agents' purpose was to do just the opposite. For example, tear gas had long been used worldwide as form of riot control. It incapacitates subjects through temporary loss of vision and a diminished ability to breathe. It is important to note that these are temporary. Short term side effects can include diarrhea, hyperthermia, etc., but long term effects are essentially non-existent. For years, tear gas was really the only option.

In the mid 1970's, there was a single, largely undocumented case of a new substance that was being tested for use in controlling unruly crowds. The riot began when a 15 year old girl, for reasons that remain largely unknown to this day, was mistakenly shot by an undercover police detective,. Her death was unwittingly captured by local news cameras. The footage was subsequently copied and distributed in the days and weeks to follow. For the first time ever the world witnessed a person of innocence dying before its' very eyes. It was played over and over again; in primetime, in living color. The death of Alisha Grugorio, the victim of blatant police arrogance, produced protests and demonstrations that eventually escalated from peaceful and civil to violent rioting. Tens of thousands of rioters damaged property and threatened the prevailing rule of law.

Law enforcement officials decided to employ the use of an untested chemical agent. Borrowed from the Soviet Union, it was called Tenkerov A23, and although unproven it was deemed necessary to take back the streets and reinstitute law and order. Tenkerov A23 was an incapacitating agent that was used to disable the rioters that were holed up in a nearby gymnasium. The chemical substance was delivered via high powered assault rifles that fired a tiny syringe. On impact, it debilitated the subject via an immediate form of sleep paralysis. At the time, little was revealed about it and any side effects of the chemical remained virtually unknown. Half of the 75 people hiding in the gymnasium perished; under a hail of gunfire they simply fell asleep, stopped breathing, and died.

The present day version that TKO was using was also untried and any clinical precautions or methods of reviving the subject, were unknown. TKO would be using a tiny poison dart instead of a miniature syringe to incapacitate a person. It was about the size of a hollow point bullet, but had a high velocity delivery system that injected the chemical on impact and caused immediate incapacitation. Used only one other time in Southeast Asia, its' long-term effects were not known. What was known was that it was immediate; it was highly effective; and it was a potential option for use in rescuing the hostages. They called it Stardust.

On that evening, the division of the FBI also had the super elite SWAT team known as the Hostage Rescue Unit. They served as the FBI's domestic counter terrorism unit and would offer tactical solutions to safely extract the victims, and kill the perpetrators.

In the Belgium Cathedral on that cold January evening there were 1200 hostages, 90 members of the FBI's TKO and HRU units, and 7 men and 7 women with automatic assault rifles and improvised explosive devices strapped to their bodies, following the orders of one depraved madman.

Carefully, Travis pushed open the darkened entrance to the cathedral, searching with laser focus for any movement or sound, all the while recalling the words scrawled on the wall at the church in Pioneer Meadows. He thought to himself, after all these many years, with so many unanswered questions, the moment had finally arrived; a moment when things finally could be set straight.

And as he entered the darkened cathedral he murmured under his breath, "*this is it…*"

Travis' mind began to drift, if only for a moment, to a place many years previous; to a situation much like the one he was facing; to circumstances just as violent and just as deadly...

Tuesday, September 3, 1963: Evelyn June Travis was discovered late in the afternoon by her son. The young boy called his mothers' name as he wandered the house looking for her. He wasn't prepared for what he found.

He was frozen with fear. Terrified, he forced himself to move and he went running out of the house to the neighbors.

Their Tudor-style house was pristine and the lawns meticulously manicured. From the street there was a curved stone walkway that led to a large front door with perfectly cropped boxwood hedges that framed it on either side. The enormous maple tree was the centerpiece of the front yard and it was accented by a variety of nicely manicured shrubs.

The walkway was an appendage to the main driveway. It ran straight from the street to the back of the house where it stopped at the detached garage. The side of the house was covered with a massive wall of climbing ivy. The door opened into service porch and ultimately the kitchen.

Inside the kitchen the ceiling fan went round and round in a wobbly fashion. It was slightly out of alignment, making it noisier than it should have been. A radio played The Albert Pion Quartets 'Funny', as if there was something to laugh about; but the whereabouts of his mother were not immediately known.

In some ways the crime scene looked like a party had taken place, yet it was obvious that it had not. There was an open bottle of Scotch on the kitchen table with two unfinished drinks; a broken glass; and an ashtray filled with half smoked cigarettes and snuffed out butts. Oddly enough there was also a deck of playing cards and a bowl of peanuts.

In the kitchen, the frying pan contained the remainder of the last cooked meal; bits and pieces bacon, still slightly warm to the touch. There was a pile dishes on the counter, including some that were curiously broken.

The master bedroom was small by modern day standards, had a closet consistent with the design style of the day, and a tiny half bath. The doors were solid panel wood with crystal door knobs, and the lathe and plaster walls gently arched at the ceiling. It was an unnaturally dark room because of the hedges and trees outside. There were clothes strewn haphazardly about the room and the radio continued to play on, oblivious to any of the chaos. On the floor near the bed was the morning newspaper, quarter folded, with the days' cross word puzzle half finished. The pencil that was used was nowhere to be found. The bed appeared to be half made and half slept in and the mirror across the room was broken. The window had also been and the screen removed from the inside. It made sense only if one was trying to get out, not in.

The bathroom was located off the central hallway and was a marvel in artistry. The door to the room was arched and the floor and part of the walls were tiled in a green and yellow geometric mosaic pattern. At the far end was a sit down vanity with a single drawer in the center and cabinets and top drawers on each side. To the left stood a large pedestal sink and across from iit was a toilet complete with an elevated tank attached to the wall with a pull chain for activation. To the right was a stately, free standing claw tub. Perched inside, with one leg hanging over the edge in an unnatural manner was the victim, Travis' mother.

The police arrived shortly after they were called, and they gathered the following evidence and information:

The victim was thin, with a sharp-featured face. She had straight, dark brown hair and black eyes. She was approximately 30 years of age; the victim worked as a bookkeeper. She was known to be aggressive and very businesslike and somewhat of a loner. She was flat on her back, one arm resting slightly above her head and the other was laying comfortably at her side. With the exception of the ligature marks on her neck, there appeared to be very little trauma the body. Rigor mortis had already begun in her hands.

She was wearing a lemon yellow dress, and a matching jacket was found several feet from the body. She was barefoot and no shoes were found at the scene.

Blood spatter was found on her dress but the source was not immediately apparent. On further inspection, there was significant bruising on her sides and back and her eyes exhibited signs of petechial hemorrhaging. Her bra was unfastened and partially removed. The nylon cord that was used in her strangulation was actually four pieces all knotted together with slipknots and then pulled tightly around her neck.

Homicide detectives arrived at the scene and the investigation was fully underway. The once quiet, typically uneventful suburban neighborhood was teaming with law enforcement officials of all kinds including the coroner.

It was as if she had been dragged across the ground. There were a small abrasions and lacerations with a small amount of blood on both heels. She had a small scar on her left shoulder that appeared to be an old stab or gunshot wound. It was difficult to tell for sure. Time of death would be impossible to determine until a full autopsy was performed.

Law enforcement officials searched the area for several hours but found nothing to aid them in their investigation. There were no incriminating fingerprints or personal effects; no tire marks or footprints, no trace or forensic material; nothing. It was as if the murderer was a ghost who had simply vanished.

The detectives also noted that the body appeared staged and the environment at the scene was left messy yet orchestrated just the same. The neighbors that were interviewed said that they didn't hear any argument or sound of a struggle; there were no cries for help, or subsequent screams; the house sat quiet through the remainder of the afternoon.

The investigators sent out the usual bulletins and made a public appeal for any information that might lead to an arrest, but no one ever came forward….

He was taken in by his aunt and uncle, who provided him with a loving environment, a good education, and a home. Travis grew to be a young man whose heart remained broken not only for the loss of his mother, but because of the manner in which she died. He would miss her every day for the remainder of his life.

His sadness turned to rage, which turned to resolve. Early on he knew what he had to do and he hoped that by being the very best law enforcement officer he could be, he would make the terrible legacy of his mothers' death as dignified as he could.

The crowd sat silently as they anticipated what would happen next. The house lights came on and from out of the shadows (backstage left and right) they came. Seven men and seven women all wearing purple and black masks; the men were heavily armed with assault rifles while the women had improvised explosive devices strapped to their bodies. Each took their position throughout the cathedral as if on cue. The men, were evil if nothing else and quite familiar in name. Travis knew them all and had been watching them for years: Andrew Vawdrey, Barnard Hache, Charles Dalison, Giles Marshall, Matthew Taylor, Stephen Vaughan, and David Carrey.

The women were unfamiliar. This was a new twist for Preacher and uncharted territory for Travis.

No longer were they called The Circle, but rather were known as the Coven of the 7 Moons, and their number was many.

They had a menacing reputation that was found throughout the world and in the belief systems of many cultures. However, the Coven of the 7 Moons was also a place; where people haunted the darker places of the underworld, ready to draft any unsuspecting wayward soul whenever the opportunity arose. Over the years it became the meeting place for evil spirits, demons and witches, and was the home of ghosts, black dogs and other supernatural phenomenon. They were stuck between two worlds, and made little or no effort to either advance or retreat from one to another.

The Coven of the 7 Moons was also the final resting place for murderers, executed criminals, suicides, and psychopathic serial killers. Most though, believed this to be mere folklore and without merit.

The legend was founded in myth that meandered its way into society and modern culture, but little was known or written about it.

The Coven of the 7 Moons was also a dogma which clearly emphasized that Godlessness is the only way to true spiritual joy, and that all other religions are nothing more than cults. There was no single manifesto that detailed this belief system, but rather a combination of writings and publications all rolled into one. Believers used the Bible solely as a means to an end, in order to promote their own agenda. For example, the Coven of the 7 Moons interpreted the Book of Genesis in a way that proclaims Adam as godhead. Furthermore, they firmly believed Eve was seduced by the snake (Satan) and gave birth to two blood lines: Cain, the direct descendent of Satan and Eve, and Able of Adam, who was godhead. As a result of this, they also believed that the Jews had been inclined to carry on the Cain blood line, and would eventually dominate the World. The core of their hatred rested in the Jewish religion and was supported with a biblical justification for their beliefs.

The Coven of the 7 Moons also believed strongly in the certainty of the end of the world and the Second Coming of Christ. It was also believed that these events were part of a purification process that was necessary before Christ's kingdom could be established on earth. The real question was; who was their Christ; who was their God? Their doctrine consistently used 'Christ' throughout, but never invoked the name of Jesus. Of course, it could not be spoken because their God was The Dark Lord; Satan. They held to the belief that during this time, Jews and their allies would attempt to destroy mankind by using any means available. The result would be a brutal and bloody resistance—a war between God's forces, and the forces of evil.

In fact, their beliefs were an irrational string of biblical pabulum, endlessly assembled to allow the innocent to believe they were a part of something divine, and in the end it was nothing more than a lie.

One by one they exited stage left and right, taking their positions along the outer perimeter of the auditorium. Preacher followed and headed toward center stage.

Suddenly Dr. Teplitz stood in outrage and approached Preacher. It was either tremendous courage or blatant stupidity that prompted him to demand a reason for their obnoxious interruption. While continuing his placid walk towards the front of the stage, never once looking in the direction of Dr. Teplitz, he pulled his out his .38, pointed it at him and fired one shot to his heart. Even though there were screams and gasps from the audience, Preacher never missed a step and just continued his walk to center stage.

He tossed the gun high up into the air and before it landed back into his hand, it was transfigured into a bouquet of deep red roses. This took the audience by surprise. The trick seemed so much like a show, that some even started to applaud. However, at the sound of such applause Preacher simply put his index finger to his tightly closed lips as if to say, "Shhh" and then tossed the bouquet of roses straight into the air. The audience was eerily silent and all eyes were fixed upon the flowers; waiting for them to drop. But they never did; the bouquet, while remaining intact and perfectly unruffled, simply hung in air, free floating.

With the wave of a hand, the body of Dr. Teplitz slid across the the polished wooden floor without aid and disappeared behind the curtain. Then with a wave of the other hand, the chair Dr. Teplitz was sitting in glided towards Preacher and seemingly on command, stopped directly behind him.

He raised his hand in the air, palm open, and 3 small rubber balls (red, blue, and black) fell from the ceiling into his hand. He began to juggle them; first with two hands in a traditional manner, then with one hand; then 2 more rubber balls fell from up above, white and green. Suddenly the balls began to juggle by themselves and each ball ignited in flames. To top it off, he caught an apple in his mouth that also fell from out of nowhere.

Preacher took a bite of the apple while sitting in the chair, admiring the red roses and the juggling balls as a matter of his handy work. A few of the Coven of the 7 Moons began to applaud; Preacher cocked his head, and with seeming approval encouraged the rest of the audience to follow suit. They reluctantly did so.

Next, he raised his hand into the air as if he was hailing a taxi, and from nowhere a sawed-off shotgun flew into his grasp. Compared to a standard shotgun, the sawed-off shotgun had a shorter gun barrel, and a stock that was more like a pistol than a rifle.

Abruptly, he did a 180° turn and made direct eye contact with Dr. Reiber, who remained sitting in his chair.

"Come here." Preacher said through transference. "And please do not act like you don't hear me…" Preacher raised the shotgun slowly.

Dr. Reiber knew that there was no bluffing Preacher. He slowly pulled himself out of the chair, and began a purposeful walk towards Preacher.

"Thank you." Preacher said in voice with a smile. "Makes things a lot easier, don't you think?" Suddenly, he struck Dr. Reiber with the barrel end of the shotgun. It hit him hard enough to knock him down, but not unconscious. As Dr. Reiber tried to pull himself up, Preacher grabbed him by the back of the collar and brought him to his knees once again.

Preacher began an elaborate process that was intended to secure his freedom and buy as much time as he thought he might need. He wired the sawed-off shotgun around Dr. Reiber's neck. The safety on the shotgun had been removed and the wire around the doctors' neck was connected to the trigger. Known as the "dead man's line", it was made in such a way that if the FBI shot

Preacher, or if Dr. Reiber fell or tried to escape, the shotgun would blow his head off.

Preacher began a lengthy diatribe in front of the live TV cameras. Agitated and extremely emotional throughout, he literally dragged Dr. Reiber from one side of the stage to the other; keeping his finger on the shotgun trigger at all times. Pulling and pushing him like a dog tethered to a stick, the wire at one point began to cut Dr. Reiber's head and a small trail of blood ran slowly down his face. At that point, unbeknownst to Preacher, the producers in the remote TV trucks were sure he was going to kill Dr. Reiber and decided to terminate the live broadcast.

Travis kept his team calm and patient, making it clear that nothing was to happen yet.

With the apple in one hand, and the shotgun tied to Dr. Reiber's head in the other, he began:

"I guess it really… all did… begin with an apple…" he said while talking with a mouthful of apple. "Actually, did you know that the Bible says 'fruit', not apple? Since the dawn of man the apple has always gotten a bad rap. Imagine being the brunt of every joke, or the reason for the original sin, forever? We're going to have quite a lot of time together this evening, so let me tell you a little about myself. They call me Preacher and these wonderful individuals are part of a flock called the Coven of the 7 Moons. With humble beginnings in 1967, they are now 20,000 members strong worldwide and growing in strength each day.

There are a lot of misconceptions about me, my team, and The Coven of the 7 Moons so I was thinking this might be a good time to set the record straight. Have you ever had something that was just so annoying that it eventually stopped bothering you altogether? Well me too; but I do worry about the message that it sends to The Coven of the 7 Moons. I feel an obligation to them, to set the record straight. I think it is because we are so many in number, what with e-mail and the internet now. Would you believe most people perceive me to be a threat; can you believe it? Oh sure, there were a couple of, shall we say, incidents. But by their own belief they are in a better place, so I am told.

You know, I spent a lot of time with some Christian Pastors, diligently trying to understand this mindless pabulum and so many of them seem so motivated by fear. Let me explain it this way; how can it be that so many seem to lack sufficient knowledge, hold on tightly to the predictions acknowledged in Revelations, and use Apocalypse as a reason to stick with God? Don't you think it's kind of overkill; this whole fear thing is really used ad nauseam…Many in Christianity have been predicting Armageddon for hundreds of years. And of course when it doesn't they become really quiet… excuses.

The truth is there are some pretty significant changes up ahead—oh I know what they are, but if I told you I'd have to kill you, so to speak. You still have plenty of time to make that next big purchase though; you know… new house, car, etc...

Back to Revelation…with a show of hands how many people here have read it? Very good. OK, also with a show of hands, how many people understood it? Ah…that's what I thought. So, let's chat a little bit about these prophecies shall we?

Human kind, since the beginning of time, has known earthquakes, famine, and pestilence. Eventually, modern science found unique ways to tame diseases with breakthrough medicines, measure earthquakes in order to evaluate the epicenters and magnitude, as well as develop technology to predict the conditions for a devastating tornado and alert the public at large. And with a media system that is not only spontaneous, but worldwide, news of such events is direct to the public with an immediacy the likes of which have never been known before. Prior to this, such events would be recorded in a local fashion, and likely would never be mentioned in any particular world class newspapers, let alone media forms that were at the time non-existent.

The end of time has always been a *real* hot topic, no pun intended, for the **Judeo—Christian** community. *Why* is somewhat of a mystery to me, because it really is fear mongering at its very height.

So, is it a Book of Myths? With legends and characters and suffering for a lost cause or series of lost causes? Or perhaps it is a Book that is a collection of stolen books? "

There were long periods of silence as Preachers' rambling would pause without reason. He would resume where he left off as if on cue. It was during one of those periods of silence that the TKO unit began to maneuver into the cathedral, make their way to the balcony, and one by one began to get into position. Their goal was simple: incapacitate the 14 members of the Coven of the 7 Moons, and eventually Preacher himself.

Travis had made his way back stage, sliding against the masonry wall of the antique building. Silently moving towards Preacher, he crept closer to the stage and could see him sitting in the chair. Travis raised the heavy .44 and took aim at Preacher's head and then whispered in the mouthpiece of his radio that the mission would proceed with incapacitation procedures. They were to employ the use of Stardust, and each member would announce a 'ready' when in position…

In the midst of all that was going on, Preacher's mind wandered for a moment and recalled a time many years prior; an innocent time before the murders had begun, when he was just a boy, standing alone in a crowd, watching. The circumstances were etched in his memory, for just a moment his eyes met those of the convicted murderer AJ Houseman. As he gazed briefly into those bright blue eyes time stopped, and Lucas was sucked in, lifted high into the air, travelling at great speeds, and peering down upon the open land below. The sky was dark; a kind of black/blue that was full of stars and cloudless. He was not afraid, even though he thought to himself that he really should be. From his position high in the sky he could see a small village far down below him. With the lights flickering like stars on the ground, he thought they must be fire or torches. He realized these were not like the lights like back in Jeff City. And as he gazed down upon the land, he sensed he was descending. Before long, he was travelling at an alarming speed but he was so energized knowing he was flying that he gave very little thought to the danger he was in. With a thud, he landed at the front gate of what appeared to be a 17th century castle. He picked himself up and went towards the door. From his vantage point he could see that some kind of meeting was going on, and he went inside to investigate. It did not take long before he realized that he was invisible to everyone else. He could see and hear them, but they seemed oblivious to his presence. From a distance he watched the curious proceeding and realized that it was a criminal trial.The Judge walked in (or what he thought was the judge) and took his seat on a raised platform at the front of court. He was an old man who spoke with a heavy Irish accent, wore white collars, a black robe and a wig. The Lord of the High court had beady gray eyes that were like two silver coins. He was bald, and short but possessed a graceful build. His skin was light-colored and he had a large nose and delicate ears.

He motioned to the sheriff to begin the proceedings. The sheriff was a peculiar man as well, whose walk was reminiscent of a strutting cat as his hips moved in and out of unison. He was hardly majestic but his wardrobe was businesslike and strange, with a completely black color scheme. He had droopy eyes the color of chestnuts, dark skin and thin lips.

Standing in front of the open court, the sheriff began:

"Before his majesty of the high court, Lord Senior Tinsley, bring forth herewith, The Examination and Confession of Abigail Alvah of Dublin, Ireland, on this day of the Lord.

The following submission is to be entered into court documents:

That the hand of one Master Brock Noble made her a witch.

That sometime last spring she agreed to the creed and subsequent laws made freely upon her by the Devil.

And as such, The Devil commanded Abigail Alvah to hurt and otherwise create the demise of those in her township, against the Lord Christ Jesus and the kingdom of Ireland.

Furthermore in order to afflict a lasting curse upon the families in Troan Oak lane, she claims in confession that she afflicted the curse by squeezing her hands.

And that she furthermore confesses she was at the witch meeting at Mula Thaerer Village.

And further the Devil told her it would be very brave and clever for her to come down here to Dublin among these accused persons. And that she should never be brought out. She promises to confess what more she shall hereafter remember.

Witness shall rise and speak when spoken to—please escort the witness to chamber…"

There was a thud and creaking noise, the kind that sounds like a wall is breaking, as the jailer opened the door. This allowed the defendant to move freely from her cell to the court room enabling the prisoner to speak directly to the Judge while remaining behind bars.

"State your name." the sheriff barked. "And how do you plead?"

"Abigail Alvah." she replied while looking away. "Innocent my Lord"

"My dear," Lord Senior Tinsley began. "How is it you manage to put forth a confession to the charges in such detail and now claim to be innocent?"

"With all due respect your Lordship," She started. "It was because that man, the sheriff, had threatened to kill my son if I did not confess. I could not to let him do that."

Lord Senior Tinsley gazed at the Sheriff, who had unknowingly fallen asleep and lightly cleared his throat. "Is this true, Sheriff?" He spoke. "Did you cause this woman to confess under duress?"

"It's an outrage, my Lord." The sheriff began while propping his portly body up from the chair. "The fact is she is lying. She lies about everything, because she has become one with Devil." There was an ugly murmur in the gallery of the court room.

Then Abigail Alvah started to laugh—an insane laugh, the laugh of someone mad, someone who had gone astray, someone lost in evil.

"Are you a witch Ms. Alvah?" Lord Senior Tinsley asked. "And did you repudiate the Lord Jesus Christ in order to worship the Devil, make pacts with him and otherwise employ demons to accomplish magical deeds?"

She stopped laughing and looked straight towards him, and said nothing.

"Have you no defense for yourself?" He asked, but no reply came. "Pity. Therefore based on your confession against the Kingdom of Ireland, for crimes against God and state, you shall be put to death for the crimes of Witchcraft and Sorcery, and shall be hanged by the neck until dead. May God have pity on your soul."

Then Abigail Alvah looked at the judge, with blood red eyes that were filled with hate. She spoke, but in a different voice and said: "I am Shamus Merlin Alvah. My heritage and religion require that we choose a new witch name for each degree of witchcraft. It is therefore, that I am an initiated 3rd High Priest of the Coven of the 7 Moons lineage. The Coven of the 7 Moons began in 1210 AD, and continues its passage in strength. It was founded by Lady Aeron Namur Alvah, who is the Celtic goddess of battle and slaughter as well as my wife; and born to us was a daughter whom you have committed to execution. Killing her will not change things to come, only alter them slightly. Killing her will only torture me; it will bring forth an onslaught of dark events and will cause certain demise throughout the land and throughout the kingdom. Therefore, my Lord, free yourself while the opportunity to do so is at hand, for if she is not released a terrible curse will fall upon you High Lord Senior Tinsley and all of your family and the entire lineage of Tinsley;

for now and forever more, for as long as the sky is blue and the grass is green, you shall be hunted and haunted and tracked down until every Tinsley known to mankind is dead. So mote it be."

She then let a soulful chilling cry and said "Curse you Lord Tinsley, curse you." And she was right, because in an instant that deep tortured cry lunged at Lord Senior Tinsley, hitting him with a jolt and causing his heart stop. And he suddenly dropped dead and fell forward onto the ornate desk, his head hitting the table top with a thud. Then in an instant Abigail Alvah burst into flames from head to toe. The jailer and the sheriff ran to her to try to open the door but it was jammed shut and would not free itself. The heat was so intense there was no way to get close enough to help her, and as quickly as it had started she lay smoldering in ashes.

Abigail Alvah was right about the curse, as was witnessed by the gallery regarding the death of Lord Senior Tinsley, but that was only the beginning. Strange things and occurrences, along with a tremendous amount of bad luck, seemed to find his family. The haunting had already begun. His eldest and only son, Thomas, went mad after telling his mother that he had seen an enormous black, headless dog and believed it to be following him wherever he went. Convinced that he was being followed and eventually chased by the beast, his mother witnessed the mental destruction of her son, deserting him in the end, by having committed him to an asylum.

Lord Senior Tinsley's wife, Agatha Tinsley, was also met with her share of challenges and those began to manifest themselves only months after she had her son committed. First, it began with a strange tingling in her legs, an almost nagging ache that was relentless. Night after night she endured severe pain and sleepless nights until it all became unbearable. Her body wore down, her skin became pale white and pasty, she had dark black circles under her eyes, and she lost a lot of weight. She was beginning the process of slowly dying. She went to many doctors for any kind of relief, but they all were perplexed in trying to come up with a treatment. Then one night it stopped, and for the first time in months she was able to sleep.

When she woke, after many hours of sleep, she did so in horror. Although there was no longer any pain, and she could walk without any problem, her legs had permanently and rapidly deformed. They were crooked and misshapen. In her shame, she went into virtual hiding and began living in the forest by day and in the cemetery by night. Thereafter it was said that anyone with crooked legs, should know she is a witch and should leave that place immediately.

Then the vision ended and Lucas once again found himself looking into the eyes of AJ Houseman who winked and smiled at him…The Thousand Year Curse had begun…

"Then life is really in a mess," Preacher started again.

"It's in such disarray that it is difficult to know which way to turn. Ask yourself a few questions, like what does the future hold for you? Do you know your future? What about your futures or the futures of others—can you foretell them? How do you stop Fate? And what role does Destiny play in your life? Can you deflect pain, diminish the aging process, or heal yourself…and what about this levitation thing anyway?

There are a handful of people who possess the capacity to alter their surroundings using the control of their mind. As a society we possess one significant element that renders us helpless against other beings: the highly developed use of their brains."

In the moments of quiet and the long periods of boredom, the hours passed slowly. The hostages were restless and continued to stir. The air in the auditorium became thick and stale, and barely breathable. Eventually everyone had to relieve themselves, but using the public restrooms located in the main entrance of the cathedral was out of the question. The only available option was the orchestra pit and a line began to form as people crawled over the rail and into pit. The stench was overwhelming and revolting, and the urine was so deep in some places it began to cover ones shoes.

Preacher looked up at the roses and they suddenly broke loose from the suspended animation. With the force 50 pounds they came plummeting down, crashed into the stage floor, and broke into small shards of colored glass. Turning to the audience, he began again…

"Most people have no knowledge of their third eye, the crown chakra, let alone the enabling or empowering of it. Although true, there are other psychic centers within us that we can use to experience this untapped realm. Reliance solely on our five senses directly influences our lives and the world around us."

One by one the juggling balls began to flame out and drop to the floor.

"However, there is one such person who has experienced her 3rd eye; her chakra and her psychic center; …and she is in this room today. It's time for us to meet at last and be properly introduced. Wherever you are Sabra—you need to make yourself known to me or I will kill your doctor friend."

Silence followed as those in the audience stretched and craned their heads looking for the unknown person. All of the TKO team had confirmed their readiness; then Travis said, "on my count…3..2..1…"

Sabra slowly rose from center right in the audience and said, "I am Sabra Tinsley Torrington", and at that moment all of TKO assault rifles, fully loaded with the incapacitating agent, simultaneously fired, and every one of them hit their targets. The audience gasped and as if choreographed to a silent musical, operatic in nature but free flowing nonetheless. Each of the members of the Coven of the 7 Moons went down. They fell one by one in a cascading manner, more like crumbling really, as the effect of the knock out drug was fast and resistance was futile.

Preacher stopped midsentence, panned from left to right and thought to himself…"Travis". He tightened his grip on the gun, and yanked Dr. Reiber's head in anger.

Travis heard Preacher and replied via thought transference; "this is it, Preacher." he thought as he tightened grip on the firearm, sharpened his aim, and waited for the right moment...

Preacher became furious. The furniture on the stage simultaneously threw itself across the theater. The audience sat in horror.

"It is so sad," he said while pointing at Sabra. "That once again, it is lost."

Without warning the lights flickered off, taking everyone, including Preacher, by surprise. He loosened his grip on the rifle just slightly as he tried to determine what was happening. The ground rumbled, moaning and groaning as if tortured with agony. The Belgium Cathedral began to shake, the timber frame creaking and splintering as if the entire structure was doomed to fall at any moment. Somewhere in the distance, perhaps in an outer building, there was the sound of breaking glass as if it was falling from many floors up. The terrified people in the audience began to scream. The floor rippled and buckled and twisted, heaving with pain, as the wild event began to slow to an end.

And for the first time in a number of years, Preacher was admittedly frightened.

The first flash of light was nothing more than a bother, but then it was followed by a second and then a third. Preacher then realized that these little flashes were not a part of the environment, spurred on by some electrical malfunction, but rather were flashes of intense white light in both of his eyes....As he continued to try to ignore them, the effect worsened. They bounced around in an unorganized manner, like a pinball machine in his head. He blinked his eyes harder and faster and became increasingly agitated. The flashes of light emitted a piercing sensation that came even faster and more furious than ever. He began to rub one of his eyes; slowly lowering the rifle so he could use both hands, and began to fiercely blink to try to focus.

The wire that had so tenuously held the gun to Dr. Reiber's head loosened. It was as if someone was unraveling it. Miraculously, the gun dropped to the floor without firing. Dr. Reiber stumbled backwards, trying to regain his balance. Eventually he fell to the floor and began crawling to the back of the stage.

For Preacher, nothing was working, and it was at this point he realized that his eyesight had been rendered useless. He was confused and frustrated and the only thing visible to him, either with eyes closed or opened, was a solid mass of immense white light. It was like some kind of aura in his head, visible to no one else. He was completely blind.

He began to feel a tingling sensation in his hands that eventually went to his arms, shoulders and face. He tried to speak but started to have problems putting the words in order. He was clearly becoming more and more frustrated. In an almost paralytic state he desperately attempted to regain control of the rifle and knelt on one knee fumbling blindly for it, unable to see or feel anything.

From inside the mobile TV truck, cameras one and two had long been stationary and any production had been halted. However, when the producer noticed the strange immobilizing antics of Preacher, he began to cue the camera into position in order to capture the moment in all of its completeness. So, the taping began again.

Preacher toiled angrily at his blindness and his inability to feel anything; he was startled when he heard a voice…a sweet voice that resonated peacefully, with love and joy.

"Sometimes a man reaches a stage in his life, at a place that often is considered the most contemplative, where the mind begins to produce torture because there is no joy or peace."

The TV producer in the mobile truck stopped in his tracks to do a double take, to hear the voice and capture it as part of the video. He had no idea where it was coming from or who it was. He cued camera 2 for a close up of Preacher, and then camera 1…

"These are the things that life has presented to you," the voice continued. "The things that gather useless dust, have little or no merit, and long only for confusion. These are not things of Love, but rather are things of hate and destruction, whose only purpose is to achieve a longing for annihilation.

Your presence has allowed an opportunity for you to change all that was, to have such an effect on the world in a positive way, but yet you have chosen to persecute me. As the result, that fight has been fought with the blood of others, and for this you have earned nothing; not respect, nor love of brother, insight, joy, or peace; nothing. But the time is now and the place is here, that we settle this long score and move on from this to a place that is better and vastly different." The Lord stopped speaking while a confused Preacher, subdued in demeanor and as lost as ever, waited for His next sentence…

Sitting next to Sabra, who remained standing although trembling with complete fear, was Stephanie LAN LAN Meng.

She was from Liuzhou, Guangxi province—southern China. She was in St. Louis in order to continue her education, and was attending the lecture for extra credit.

It was quite by chance when she was invited to a Chinese Christian church in Beijing—the main selling attraction was not God or the promise of eternal life, but rather it was the free English courses they offered. Unbeknownst to Stephanie, indeed the main attraction was God, only He would be revealed in other ways. It was through this connection to God that the Holy Spirit came upon Stephanie, and from that humble beginning her prayers were indeed answered. She would find herself studying abroad, in St. Louis, and find herself in the Belgium Cathedral sitting next to the one person in the audience that the psychotic madman on the stage was so determined to destroy. It was clear to her that she was there for only one reason. Stephanie stood up and took Sabra's hand…and they held on tightly…

Preacher knelt down in complete torture, and cried out "this cannot be happening to me?" Unknown to Preacher, everyone in the auditorium could hear The Lord speak, not only Preacher, and silently and reverently everyone listened.

Mobile TV truck 2—'cue camera 3 and 4…pan audience sweep right…'

"I am, Lucas; I am..." The Lord began. "I am enlightenment, explanation, revelation, and illumination; I am love, tenderness, warmth, and friendship; I am healer, restorer, and reconciler; I am counselor, director, and leader; I am spirit, strength, and courage; I am passion, zeal, and delight; I am truth, integrity, and veracity; I am honesty, reality, and loyalty; I am genuineness, dedication, and sincerity; I am omnipotent, all-powerful, supreme, and invincible; I am Redemption, salvation, deliverance, and surrender.

Heaven is love, sanctuary, protection. There is no pain, no lies, no death, no tears, no poverty, no greed, and no crimes. Heaven is joy, song, laughter, friendship. There are no demons, no dark Angels, no mysticism, no threat of war or rumors of war.

And this is how it is Lucas…the comparison of this life to Heaven, is no comparison at all…

Because, on the one hand—there is love, on the other there is hate.

On the one hand—there is healing, on the other there is sickness.

On the one hand—there is joy, on the other there is sadness

On the one hand—there is reconciliation, on the other there is condemnation

On the one hand—there is vision, on the other there is blindness

On the one hand—there is reception, on the other there is deception

On the one hand—there are no tears, on the other there is nothing but tears

On the one hand—there is no fear; on the other fear is the great motivator

On the one hand—there is eternal life, on the other there is eternal hell. Which hand shall you choose Lucas?

You speak eloquently of the other Gods, as you put it. Buddha, Confucius, Mohammed all professed great things, were no doubt scholarly men, and were perhaps men of Wisdom and insight. However, they all shared a common thread; they died, and not one of them came back to life from the dead. Their religions continue to profess that they must await the coming of The Messiah; they are still waiting Lucas, and for an eternity to come they shall continue their wait. They did not return; I did. I was murdered and rose from the dead for the eternal glory of the

Father, to bear the burden of the sins of all mankind and defeat death forever.

All of these are people who are part of history; I am a history maker.

Facts are much different than truth, Lucas. Facts are represented by the things of this world; life, debt, illness, death, unemployment, money. Truth is heaven, forgiveness, light, love, God. John 3:16—For God so loved the world—it is the antithesis argument for elaboration and is designed not for Christians, not for Baptists, not to satisfy doctrine, not for other religions; but for you. All of what I am is for you."

"Lucas," the Lord said. "How I have loved you so and continue to love to this very day, hour and minute. Evil has always been intriguing and compelling to you, as it is the element that has drawn you in. You have taken every opportunity to shun me and have only yourself to blame. But I do not blame you; I love you; I forgive you; I choose you.

From this day forward you will choose a life of evil and sinfulness no more; and the remainder of your life, regardless of the capacity or incapacity, shall be spent working in my Name; to keep those more vulnerable and younger than you away from the Darkness, the madness, and the lost ways that enslave you now."

"I have hurt so many Lord," Preacher said looking aimlessly towards the intense white light. "I can never repay; I am never going to be worthy; why would you waste your time on me? I have killed and maimed, no one could or would want to love me Lord."

Then Jesus said, "There are 3 principles you must follow Lucas: Use what you have, do what you can, and start where you are.

I created you, Lucas. I do not wish to see destroyed the things I love and have created. I love you, and you are worthy—You will leave this life of hate and evil, and you will sin no more. You will spend your remaining days working in my Name to the benefit of all creation, so they do not fall victim to the same lies that you did."

Mobile truck 1—cue camera 2; pan close up Preacher, and cue camera 1…

With Stephanie standing beside Sabra, she began to sing Amazing Grace; the sweetest, softest, kindest voice could be heard echoing throughout the auditorium. Throughout the giant hallway and in the arched foyer: in the grand office and upstairs; from the sidewalk outside and down to the basement. It resonated with pure love of the Lord. Then Sabra soon joined in, and a few people in the back stood to sing as well. Before long, everyone was on their feet singing; the old, the young, the married and the single; from all races and types of backgrounds; their voices carried throughout the Belgium Cathedral like a well rehearsed choir. And suddenly the dire circumstances and violence of the hostage crisis was forgotten, if only for a moment, and replaced with a joy that was perfected by God.

Preacher remained on his knees, raised his head toward The Lord and with eyes closed and arms outstretched, and tears streaming down his face he said; "Lord Jesus please, please forgive me. I love you, Lord, I love you."

In that moment a depraved madman, one who had created so much death and sorrow in so many lives, for so many years, was forgiven. He had become the property of God now and no matter the consequences for his actions in this lifetime, he now belonged to Jesus.

At that moment, the intense white light that had blinded him completely began to dissipate and vanish, and while tears streamed down his face, his sight was restored to original.

Travis slowly walked behind him, handcuffed him without resistance, and began to lead him away. He asked Travis if he could at least meet Sabra…it was then, of course, that he told Preacher of the deception: Sabra was actually Agent Shelly Duncan of the FBI TKO unit; she was used in place of the real Sabra as a decoy since they knew that he would be there, and likely attempt to take her life.

Preacher was led away in shackles to a nearby car and whisked out sight to a holding cell..

At 7:00 a.m., rescuers began helping the hostages out of The Belgium Cathedral. Most were led to safety, but a few were not so lucky. The 11 hour ordeal took its toll on two elderly victims who succumbed to heart attack and stroke. All 14 members of the Coven of the 7 Moons died. The bodies were laid in rows on the foyer and on the pavement at the main entrance to the cathedral, exposed to a light rain that eventually turned into snow. None of the bodies had wounds or showed signs of blood loss or trauma, but their faces were a pasty white and their limbs had atrophied; their eyes were opened and fixed.

Most of the terrorist group choked to death on their own vomit or just stopped breathing shortly after being hit by the knock out drug. The effects of the paralyzing agent were so intense that it slowed down normal bodily functions to the point where they simply stopped working. Medical workers were expecting to treat victims of explosions and gunfire but not a secret chemical agent, and as such were unprepared.

The bodies of dead terrorists were eventually carried to a waiting bus, which was parked just outside the main entrance to the cathedral. These casualties remained nameless; their identities were a well guarded secret for a relatively long period of time. Initial reports said nothing about who they were, what their motivation was, creed, doctrine, etc. They were moved away so quickly and out of public view. In the fray and excitement of the moment all of the attention was elsewhere, and no one noticed. Eventually, the names of those who lost their lives were released with little or no fanfare from the media, and were barely noticed at all.

Everyone was eventually led out of the building to safety, and the hostage crisis at The Belgium Cathedral ended without further incident.

Inside the mobile TV truck, the producer and staff began to review the magnificent video where they captured a full confession, rebuking and forgiveness all from The Lord Jesus on prime time. They rewound the video to the place where the Lord began to speak to Preacher, but it was silent and the only voice that could be heard, sporadically at best, was Preachers'. They watched and listened in disbelief. This miraculous event, greater than anything they had ever seen before, would not be for sale as a marketing event; it would not garner a Nobel Peace prize or an Emmy or an Oscar; it would not become an award winning documentary. It however would be an event that changed the lives of everyone who was present, forever.

That days' newspaper, the only one in Pioneer Meadows, ran and re-ran the only major story that mattered to its' readers; the sad and unfortunate death of Rev. Mary Richards Tinsley.

8. Reconciliation

Some weeks later, Travis sat quietly on the bench in front of the hospital entrance, smoking a cigarette and balancing a cup of coffee with his newspaper. It all read as planned. Once again Travis had managed to send the press down the wrong road when it came to the Church Assassin, as he had done all those many years.

St. Mary's Hospital in Pioneer Meadows sat off the main highway. Picturesque, unobtrusive, well maintained, and quiet: all of the elements necessary for healing. The facility opened in 1906, at a time when Pioneer Meadows had begun to thrive. The opening of the first medical care facility in the tri-city region meant not having to travel many miles to one of the larger cities. It was welcomed by all.

The automatic doors swished open and closed without prompting, as if a playful ghost was passing by the infrared sensor that activated it. There was no one there, even though for a single moment Travis cocked his head away from the paper and thought, "Preacher?" and then shook it off lightly as nothing more than wind.

He stood to collect himself, knowing that he was a little late, not even sure that he should even go through with the whole thing. He walked toward the doors and as they opened he tossed the newspaper into the trash; it was something he would no longer need. He made his way to the elevator and up to room 317. On arriving, he knocked softly. Dr. Reiber opened the door quietly and motioned him to come in.

For the first time in so many years, since the time he saw Richard Tinsley's body strung up at Jesusland and all of those who were innocently killed after that, he realized that it was over. A weight was lifted from him, as he looked toward the ceiling and silently gave thanks to God.

Pastor Mary Richards Tinsley had never died: the story had been fabricated by Travis in order to throw off Preacher and it worked very well indeed. He had significant experience in spinning a story for the press, so they bought it and the rest was history.

Dr. Reiber had taken the real Sabra Tinsley Torrington to the hospital to reunite with her mother. They laid arm in arm; tears flowing freely from both. They embraced tightly but spoke no words, there was no need to; all they needed were their thoughts and that was sufficient enough for a lasting conversation.

Mary told her beautiful daughter about the struggle to give her up for adoption and that it was the most difficult thing she had ever done. But she knew Preacher would seek her; it was his destiny to do so because of the curse. Preacher also knew that if he found Sabra's mother then he would find her too, or so he believed. So, in her love for Sabra she gave her up—she never stopped loving her and never stopped believing they would one day be together again.

And on a cold December night, in an old relic of a cathedral, with so many ghosts and bad tales that it was destined for pure evil, in a place in the heart of the country, in full view of an audience, Gods' grace, the sevenfold spirit, the holy spirit, The One who was, and is, and is to come, made sure their reunion was a reality…

Travis and Dr. Reiber quietly left the room, as mother and daughter reunited, knowing that their work was complete...

Preacher was convicted of multiple murders in various states. The first trial began with the State of California for the Massacre at Jesusland. It was a short trial, because Preacher plead no contest to 48 counts of premeditated murder, confessing openly to everything.

While awaiting his first trial he was lying on his cot in solitary confinement, and remembered how badly he was treated when he first arrived at the children's orphanage. In recalling that moment he became angry and a flush of memories came to him; memories that were anger and hate filled and driven by Satan himself. Suddenly, he remembered the things that caused such terrific grief, and placed his hand to his head and began to sob. His pain, though real and tough to ignore, bore a hole into his heart that took a lifetime to create and he realized it would take a long time to find the good in it. The good of course, was God as well as the Holy Spirit that engaged him every day.

On December 30 at the Belgium Cathedral his life consisted of a legacy that was awash in hatred. Since then his battle for righteousness had indeed been won. The pain of being told that he would always be a loser, he was nothing but trouble, and that he would surely be in and out of prison, were over. There was nothing left to prove; there never was.

Since his conversion there was a new zeal for life, one that made him want to excel and be more than he ever had been. In this way, his intelligence and the act of learning had become much more disciplined than ever before. Before his transformation he never read a book, and now had suddenly turned into someone who could not get enough to read. Of course of one of thousands of books he read and re-read was the Bible. As a matter of fact, in the nearly 12 months in solitary confinement he had read the bible front to back no less than 15 times. His conversion armed him with leadership skills that he knew he had, but never before used for positive means, much less to the glory of God.

Now it seemed he no longer meandered through the days, aimless and without merit or meaning; there was a plan of sorts and it had purpose; but predominantly, there was God. Some of the days were not pleasant and some were harsh and painful. But by returning regularly to the personal sermon he cherished from the Lord, no pain was too great to endure.

In the course of those many months in solitary confinement, he chose to pen the story of his reconciliation at the Belgium Cathedral in the hopes that it might touch someone in a way that he never had before. No matter the outcome of the trial, he believed that he would, rightfully so, be put to death, and had plenty of time to prepare himself for that for that outcome. "Thy will be done." He thought to himself. Either way it was okay.

The book he wrote, a memoir really, was a detailed outline of his unexpected and impromptu meeting with Jesus at the Belgium Cathedral. Although a relatively simple book, its' contents were far reaching and deep, and it was not without its measure of pain for sure. But the pain was worth it in the long run. The chronicle of his meeting with Jesus, never before seen in modern times; witnessed by many, was breathtaking, exhilarating, and exhausting. When he finished it, he asked one of the guards he had befriended if he would like to read it. He agreed. A few days later he brought it back and told Preacher how much he had enjoyed it, and in doing so tears came to his eyes when he spoke of his beautiful encounter with the Lord. Then Preacher asked him if he would mind taking it to the Chaplain and ask him to read it as well. He had the same reaction as the guard. The Chaplain wanted to make and distribute copies to other inmates for the prison church, and Preacher agreed asking only that if any of them were ever sold the proceeds should go to his victims' families directly and nothing to himself, his heirs, or anyone else for that matter. The Chaplain agreed. His book was entitled; "My Name is Lucas; a Life Sentence".

During the trial the lead prosecutor summarized the entire 30 plus years and the ensuing killing spree efficiently and without hesitation; like a well-written script and a perfectly rehearsed play, where every word and sentence was spoken with clarity and vigor, the placement of the actors was orchestrated to the directors' liking, a cast that supported protagonist and antagonist alike; describing in detail the proverbial train wreck that Preachers life had been.

Then the judge asked him if he wanted to make statement before sentencing, he nodded yes. For a moment he looked down and then stared up at the ceiling with a slight grin: "Where do I start Lord." He began. "Your honor I wish to start by saying I am truly sorry for all of the pain and suffering I have caused, and really nothing that I can say or do can change that now. But I would if I could; not for me but those families of the victims that are left behind. The only thing I can say is that a lonely, selfish prideful man stood on a stage in St. Louis and experienced The Lord in a way that I could never explain; I could never understand; and can only be thankful that He did. Not that anyone would really understand me, truthfully I don't understand myself most of the time, but I was a changed person, and whatever is the will of God, is my will also. I will not hesitate to make it right, either in what remains of my life in Earth, or in my execution. Thank you for your time and God Bless."

…Over the next 2 years, his book became a best seller, went on to be printed and distributed in 36 countries worldwide, and was nominated for The Spencer Book Award.

…The State of California, as well as Colorado, Wyoming, Montana and Texas, found him guilty of premeditated murder and sentenced him to death by lethal injection. He waived all of his appeals and remained on death row in California…

3 years later…

Preacher made the difficult walk from his cell to the death chamber, guided between two guards and flanked by the prison Chaplain and Warden. It would be the last walk he would make. On that walk, The Lord spoke to him and that made the task a little more bearable.

"Grace," The Lord said to Preacher. "is what I give when all you have is your faith. The more you depend on me, the more grace I give. Depend on Me. Remember, I always love you".

And with that, Preacher knew he had come home at last…

2 Corinthians 5

(New International Version)

[17]Therefore, if anyone is in Christ, he is a new creation; the old has gone, the new has come! [18] All this is from God, who reconciled us to himself through Christ and gave us the ministry of reconciliation.

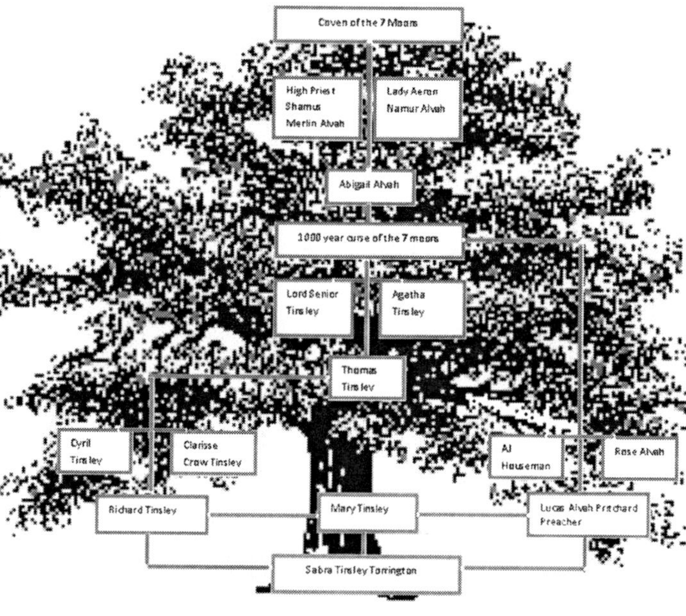

Coven of the 7 Moors
High Priest Shamus Merlin Alvah
Lady Aeron Namur Alvah
Abigail Alvah
1000 year curse of the 7 moors
Lord Senior Tinsley
Agatha Tinsley
Thomas Tinsley
Cyril Tinsley
Clarisse Crow Tinsley
Al Houseman
Rose Alvah
Richard Tinsley
Mary Tinsley
Lucas Alvah Pritchard Preacher
Sabra Tinsley Torrington

CPSIA information can be obtained at www.ICGtesting.com
260638BV00001B/124/P

9 781448 955312